Y

D0340825

Titles in The Bizarre Baron Inventions

Praise for

The Magnificent Flying Baron Estate

"Kids will want to come along for this action-packed flight as Waldo defines his true character and learns how to be his best self."

—*Story Monsters Ink*

"*The Magnificent Flying Baron Estate* is an enjoyable old-school Western with a contemporary feel . . . kids aged 9-12 are bound to enjoy this topsy-turvy tale with its funny moments of slapstick comedy."

—*The Children's Book Review*

Praise for

The Splendid Baron Submarine

"Delightfully absurd, imaginative, and fun, W.B.'s adventures will make for great read-aloud fare."

—*Foreword Reviews, Starred Review*

"Fans of the first book will be eager to read this sequel."

—*School Library Journal*

THE BIZARRE BARON INVENTIONS

THE WONDERFUL BARON DOPPELGÄNGER DEVICE

Eric Bower

Amberjack Publishing

New York | Idaho

AMBERJACK
P U B L I S H I N G

Amberjack Publishing
1472 E. Iron Eagle Dr.
Eagle, Idaho 83616
http://amberjackpublishing.com

Publisher's Cataloging-in-Publication data available upon request.
Names: Bower, Eric, author.
Title: The Wonderful Baron Doppelganger device / by Eric Bower
Series: The Bizarre Baron Inventions
Description: New York, NY; Eagle, ID: Amberjack Publishing, 2018.
Identifiers: ISBN 978-1-944995-51-5 (Hardcover) | 978-1-944995-52-2 (ebook) | LCCN 2017946708
Summary: When someone gets ahold of the Barons' Wonderful Doppelgänger Device, they use it to become a copy of W.B. to steal his parents' amazing inventions.
Subjects: LCSH Inventors--Juvenile fiction. | Inventions--Juvenile fiction. | Cloning--Juvenile fiction. | Arizona--History--19th century--Juvenile fiction. | Adventure and adventurers--Juvenile fiction. | United States--History--19th century--Juvenile fiction. | Science fiction. | Adventure fiction. | Steampunk fiction. | BISAC JUVENILE FICTION / Action & Adventure / General | JUVENILE FICTION / Steampunk | JUVENILE FICTION / Science & Technology
Classification: LCC PZ7.B6758 Bi 2017 | DDC [Fic]--dc23

Cover Design & Illustrations: Agnieszka Grochalska

Printed in the United States of America

For Brigitte & Curt, the real M & P.

TABLE OF CONTENTS

My Pants Proved How Wrong I Was By Falling To the Floor

November 13ᵗʰ, 1891

"**I**'m the real me! He's the fake W.B.!" I shouted, pointing at the fake me.

"No, I'm the real me! He's the fake W.B.!" the fake W.B. shouted, pointing at me.

Well, now I'm out of ideas.

P frowned as he looked at me, then he looked at the fake me, then at me again, then at the fake me again, and then he looked at his horse Geoffrey and smiled.

"I really love our new horse," he told my mother.

"McLaron, please focus!" M ordered.

"Right," P said as he turned back to me and the fake W.B. "W.B. and . . . *other* W.B., there is only one way to be certain which one of you is telling the truth."

He held up a funny looking device that resembled a combination between an alarm clock and a wedge of cheese.

"This," he announced, "is my newest invention. It is called the Gänger-Doppel Device. And what does the Gänger-Doppel Device do, you ask? Well, I'll tell you. It reverses the effects of my Doppelgänger Device, which is the invention that turned one of you into a perfect copy of my son. All I need to do is point the Gänger-Doppel Device at you and press this button, and then the fake W.B. will be transformed back into whoever he or she really is."

I looked over at the fake W.B. He was beginning to sweat. But then again, he looked exactly like me, and I tend to sweat a lot.

In fact, I felt my forehead and realized that I was sweating too.

"Why are you touching my forehead?" the fake W.B. asked me.

Oops. We look so much alike that even *I'm* confused about which one is the real me.

"Sorry."

"Go ahead and use the Gänger-Doppel Device on them, McLaron," M told P as she nervously clutched his arm. "I want my son back."

P frowned. Then he looked at Geoffrey and smiled again.

In P's defense, Geoffrey really was a clever horse. We were all quite fond of him.

M tweaked P's nose, and he once again focused on me and the fake me.

"There is a *slight* problem with this invention, Sharon," P told M. "You see, if you use the Gänger-Doppel Device on someone who hasn't had the Doppelgänger Device used on them first, it will try to reverse and undo who they are, which can't be done, since they already are who they are. Understand?"

"Huh?" I said.

"Huh?" the fake me said.

I'm glad that the fake me was just as confused as the real me. Otherwise, I would have been rather embarrassed. I may be slow, but at least I'm as slow as myself. I nervously ran my fingers through my hair.

"Why are you running your fingers through my hair?" the fake me asked.

"Sorry. I thought it was my hair."

"What are you saying, McLaron?" M asked P. "What happens if you use this Gänger-Doppel Device on the real W.B. instead of the fake W.B.?"

"Basically, what I'm trying to say," P said as he nervously licked his lips, "is that if I use it on the real W.B., it will turn his skin inside out."

???

. . .

!!!

For a moment, no one spoke.

I wasn't certain of many things, but I was pretty darn certain that I didn't want to have my skin turned inside out. I was actually quite used to having it outside in, or right side out, or whatever it's called when your skin is the way that it's supposed to be. I didn't know what would happen to a person who had their skin turned inside out, but I imagined that it wouldn't be too pleasant. At the very least, it would be terribly messy.

Are you confused?

You look confused. You're scratching your head more than usual, which means you're either confused, or you forgot to wash the soap out of your hair during your bath. Don't feel bad. I do that all the time.

Maybe I should start at the beginning. I'm currently at the end, where things aren't going too well for me, and if I start at the beginning, maybe you'll understand why.

My name is Waldo Baron, but since I consider Waldo to be the second worst name in the world, I prefer to be called W.B. instead. My parents, who I call P and M, are two of the cleverest inventors who have ever lived. They used to have an assistant named Rose Blackwood (who happens to be the little sister of Benedict Blackwood, the worst criminal in the history of history) who lived with us, but because of an incident involving the Doppelgänger Device, Rose decided to quit working for my parents and moved out.

Actually, she was arrested and put in jail, but I'll get to that later.

We live in a large home just outside of Pitchfork, Arizona Territory, and we call our home the Baron Estate. We live there with my Aunt Dorcas, who has what I consider to be the first worst name in the world. She is a weepy and frumpy woman, who is bothered and annoyed by every-thing. But once you get past all her whining and crying and complaining and off-key singing, she's really . . . alright, she's still pretty awful. But there isn't anything that I can do about it.

You know what? I just realized that if I start from the very beginning, I'll need to tell you about a whole lot of unimportant stuff. Let me skip to a few weeks before the Doppelgänger Device ruined our lives. That lousy inven-tion is the reason why I'm currently standing at the edge of a cliff with a fake W.B. who is claiming to be the real me. It's also the reason why there's now a fifty-fifty chance that my father will press a button on his new invention that will cause my skin to turn inside out.

You see, it all began six weeks ago . . .

The entire class pointed at me and laughed.

Most of my stories start with a large group of people pointing at me and laughing. I suppose I should be upset by that, but, to tell you the truth, it's kind of nice that I've given so many people joy. At least they don't all point at me and cry. That would be depressing.

"Class, please don't laugh at Waldo," my teacher Miss Danielle said as she sighed and gently rubbed her eyes.

I winced. I'd rather be covered in honey and dropped on an anthill than be called Waldo, and I'm not exaggerating one bit by saying that. You might be telling yourself that I'm underestimating how horrible it would be to *actually* be dropped on an anthill while covered in honey. But just last week I really *was* covered in honey and dropped onto an anthill, so I know exactly what I'm talking about.

In case you're wondering who did that to me, it was me. I accidentally did it to myself. I was making myself a bacon and honey sandwich, accidentally fell out of the kitchen window, rolled down a hill, and ended up covered in honey and ants.

I'm what you might call a little bit clumsy.

Alright, that's a lie. I'm what you might call insanely, ridiculously, unbelievably, comically, bafflingly, astonishingly, horribly, wonderfully, incomparably, undeniably, bewilderingly, extremely, astoundingly, unforgivably clumsy . . . and even *that* is letting me off a bit easy. I'm the sort of kid who, while he's asleep in bed, will accidentally roll out of a second story window, and then land on a horse that bucks him into a swamp, where he'll drop into an alligator's open mouth, and then be coughed up into a raging river, which ends in a fifty-foot waterfall drop.

That actually happened to me last month, when my family visited the state of Louisiana. It was not a highlight of the trip. In fact, after I dropped off the edge of that waterfall, I experienced very few highlights. I spent the rest of my time in Louisiana with so many bandages wrapped around me that I looked like a mummy. All I could do was lie there and moan, wishing that the accident had happened closer to Halloween.

Anyway, the children were all laughing at me because our teacher had asked us each to give an oral report on what we did over the weekend. My teacher really likes assigning us reports to present to the class but, for some reason, she never seemed to enjoy hearing mine. I guess it's because I often give reports about the adventures that I have with my inventor parents and their assistant, Rose Blackwood. And I suppose that our adventures must sound a bit ridiculous to most people. They sound pretty ridiculous to me as well. If I wasn't there to experience them, there's no way I'd believe they were real. In fact, even though I had been there to experience them, I'm still not 100 percent certain that they were real.

Suddenly, there was knocking at the schoolhouse door.

As Miss Danielle went to answer the door, I slipped for

no reason and bumped my head on the edge of her desk, before scurrying back to my seat in the corner of the room. Why did I slip and bump my head? I don't know. You might as well ask me why the grass is green, why the sky is blue, and why you get that gross, crusty stuff in the corners of your eyes after a good night's sleep.

I know that there are perfectly reasonable scientific answers to all those questions. But I don't know them, just as I don't know why it is that I happen to be the clumsiest two-legged creature on planet Earth.

The whole class watched with interest as Miss Danielle opened the schoolhouse door. We never had visitors in the middle of the day.

Standing in the open doorway, with a stack of books in his hands, was a short kid with curly black hair. Even though he was dressed the same way that most of us were dressed, the other kids in class all turned to each other to whisper about how funny looking the new kid was.

I turned and pretended to whisper to my friends too, even though I don't have any friends, and, even if I did, I would have nothing to whisper to them. I didn't think the new kid was particularly funny looking. He just looked like any other kid. To be honest, he looked boringly average, like the sort of kid who would easily blend into the crowd while walking down the street. It wasn't as though he had an eye patch or a mustache or a wooden nose or something.

"Class," Miss Danielle said, as she led the new kid to the front of the schoolhouse, "this is Belford Eustace Nigel Egbert Doolittle Ignatius Cattermole Threepwood Whitestone the Third. He will be joining our class. Please make him feel welcome."

That was our cue to give the new student a round of applause, but our hands were all frozen in shock, as we stared in disbelief at the poor kid who sounded as though he had been named after the entire British army.

I suppose Waldo wasn't that bad of a name after all.

The new kid's cheeks turned as red as a freshly picked apple.

"Actually," he said to Miss Danielle, as he cleared his throat, "if you don't mind, I prefer to be called B.W."

I smiled.

"Nonsense," said Miss Danielle as she led B.W. to his new seat. "You have a perfectly wonderful name, Belford Eustace Nigel Egbert Doolittle Ignatius Cattermole Threepwood Whitestone the Third. In fact, I quite like saying it. It's sort of like a tongue twister. I wonder if I can say it five times fast. Belford Eustace Nigel Egbert Doolittle Ignatius Cattermole Threepwood Whitestone the

Third, Belford Eustace Nigel Egbert Doolittle Ignatius Cattermole Threepwood Whitestone the Third, Beltnerd Birdsnest Egnelforp . . . oh drat. Let me try again. Belford Eustace Nigel Egbert Doolittle—"

While our teacher entertained herself by repeating the new kid's name as quickly as she could, B.W. sat beside me and took a shy glance at the rest of the class. The other children continued to whisper about him, taking the time to point and chuckle so B.W. would know for certain that they were whispering about him.

"Why are they doing that?" B.W. whispered to me.

"I don't know," I whispered back.

"Oh. Do you know what they're saying?"

"I'm not sure. I've never been a part of the whispers before. Maybe they're discussing the best way to hide their webbed toes and hairy backs during the summertime?"

B.W. giggled. "Maybe. Or maybe they're discussing the most effective way of using their thumbs to remove their earwax?"

I snickered. "Or maybe they're discussing—"

"Waldo Baron and Belford Eustace Nigel Egbert Doolittle Ignatius Cattermole Threepwood Whitestone the Third, stop whispering to one another," Miss Danielle ordered. "Otherwise, I'll have to separate you two."

I looked over at B.W. and smiled. He looked back at me and smiled as well.

Nothing helps two kids become friends like getting into trouble together.

When the teacher announced that class was over, the other children quickly poured out of the schoolhouse. B.W. and I were the last two students left. That's because B.W. was being given a special homework assignment by Miss Danielle, and I had somehow managed to get my belt stuck in my desk.

"I am assigning you an oral report to give to the class tomorrow," Miss Danielle was telling B.W. "I expect your report to last at least thirty minutes."

"Does it matter how slowly I speak?" B.W. asked.

Miss Danielle thought for a moment.

"No. I suppose it doesn't. But I want your report to include a full description of where you used to live, the school you used to attend, what you like to do for fun, what your parents do for a living, and what you would like to accomplish while here at Pitchfork School."

"All of that?" B.W. asked with a frown. "But what if I

can't remember some of those things?"

"You could just make them up?" I suggested while I tugged at my belt.

"Absolutely not!" Miss Danielle loudly declared, turning up her nose in disgust as though I had just suggested B.W. go on a cross-country crime spree. "If you tell lies, as your friend W.B. often does when he gives his ridiculous reports about his family, you will become well acquainted with the corner of the classroom, as well as the inside of the dunce cap."

She went to the closet and pulled out the dunce cap so she could show it to B.W. It was a long, pointy cap that had "DUNCE" written on it, and the inside of the cap was shaped exactly like my head. It was shaped like my head because my head was quite familiar with that cap. I wore it almost every day.

"It's not so bad," I told B.W. "It keeps your head warm in the winter."

B.W. laughed. He thought I was joking. But just wait until winter comes along, and we'll see who the one with the cold head is. It's not going to be me.

"W.B., will you please unhook your belt from your desk and go home," Miss Danielle said, then she sighed. "While I'm happy you finally made a friend, I hope you two won't turn out to be bad influences on one another."

I looked at B.W.

B.W. looked at me.

My teacher was right. I had finally made a friend at school. After all those years of the other children treating me like something brown and slimy they'd found stuck to the bottom of their shoes, I finally had someone on my side, someone who wouldn't point and laugh at me, someone I could whisper to while the other children were whispering as well, someone who could warn me if another kid was stuffing a rat into my book bag or slipping itching powder into my socks or locking me in the closet with a pack of angry dogs. I didn't understand how B.W. and I could be bad influences on one another. I finally had a friend in town, and the new kid had his first friend in Pitchfork.

What could be wrong with that? Nothing, I thought to myself. *Nothing could be wrong with that.*

Looking back, I realize that I've never been wronger about anything in my life. And I've had some impressive moments of being pretty darn wrong.

"Absolutely not," I told the teacher, as I undid my belt so I could unhook it from my desk. "We'll be good, Miss Danielle, I promise. We won't be any trouble at all. Everything will be alright."

And as Miss Danielle turned around to erase the black-board, my pants proved how wrong I was by falling to the floor.

WHY WOULD A HORSE WANT SEQUINS ON ITS HAT?

I asked B.W. if he wanted to come over to my house after school. He told me that he'd like that, and that his father wouldn't mind if he got home a little bit later than expected. So we made the long walk together, over the sandy dunes of the Pitchfork Desert, back to the only home I'd ever known: the Baron Estate.

As we walked, I told B.W. all about my family. I let him know that my parents were very brilliant and very odd inventors, which meant that he should prepare himself for a very strange afternoon. Last month, a kid had come over after school so we could work on a report together, and when he saw my father using one of his newest and weird-est inventions (the invention he called his "Mecha-Trunk":

a long, mechanical tube he attached to his nose and mouth, which he could use to suck up and shoot water, like an elephant's trunk), the kid had run away screaming. It wasn't the first time that someone had run away from the Baron Estate while screaming, and I'm pretty sure that it wouldn't be the last. People are frightened of things they don't understand, and even though I've lived with my parents all my life, I can't say that I understand them particularly well either. But I'm used to them, so I don't get frightened when I see them acting strangely. Frankly, I don't have much of a choice.

I liked B.W., so I gave him a fair warning. I told him that while he's at the Baron Estate, he should expect the unexpected. And by that, I meant that he should expect to see some baffling and crazy things, like maybe my mother using our Bigging Machine to make herself as tall as a mountain, or my father testing a pair of mechanical legs that allowed him to run as fast as a cheetah.

While some kids might have been confused or upset by that, B.W. was actually excited at the idea of seeing some of my parents' wacky inventions.

"Really?" he said. "That's fantastic! Do you think they'd let me try out one of their inventions? I've always been interested in science."

"You have?" I asked with a frown, unable to hide my disappointment.

Don't get me wrong. I like science. Science is wonderful. It's great. It's wonderfully great.

But there's something about science that my brain doesn't quite understand. My parents will sit down and try to explain their scientific inventions to me, but my brain refuses to listen. It will shut off and play loud, wacky music, usually with a lot of funny sounding horns and an off-key piano. And if I try to listen to my parents' scientific explanations despite the wacky music playing in my head, my brain will start throwing odd thoughts at me, odd thoughts which distract me. My brain will make me wonder how many hard-boiled eggs I can fit in my mouth at a time or if chipmunks are just squirrels without tails or why my belly button is so much deeper than everyone else's or what another word for "thesaurus" is.

Basically, my brain does not want me to understand science. I don't know why. I honestly don't. If you want a better answer than that, then you'll have to ask my brain. But I should warn you, it's pretty hard to get a straight answer out of it. I've been trying to get straight answers out of my brain for years.

"Of course," said B.W. with a proud grin. "I've always

wanted to be an inventor."

My face must have showed my utter disappointment that my new friend would likely be far more interested in my parents than in me, because B.W. laughed and patted me on the back.

"Don't worry, W.B.," he said. "I'm not *obsessed* with science. I just think it's fun and interesting, that's all. But I'm a normal kid who thinks that other things are fun too."

"Like what?" I asked, as I realized that I had no idea what "normal" kids did for fun.

B.W. shrugged his shoulders.

"I don't know. Shooting at tin cans. Pretending we're bandits at the bank. Playing Hull Gull with beans. The usual games kids play."

I'd never shot a tin can with anything before. And I've never pretended to be a bandit at the bank—what was I supposed to do, tie a bandana over my nose and mouth and then pretend to open a savings account? And I had absolutely no idea what a *Hull Gull* was, or why on earth you played it while eating beans. Could I play it while eating cornbread and sausage too? If so, then I think I liked Hull Gull the best out of all those options.

But the last thing I wanted was for my first friend in Pitchfork to think I didn't know what normal kids did. So

I nodded my head quickly with a big, fake smile plastered on my face.

"Yeah, me too," I said. "Bandit banking. Shooting cans with . . . things. Eating bean games. I like doing all that stuff too. I certainly don't spend all of my time sitting in bed, reading adventure novels while eating pie."

I was a bit surprised when we arrived at the Baron Estate and nothing odd appeared to be happening. There were no explosions or fires or gigantic metal contraptions that would turn you into a bird if you flipped a metal switch. There were no flying machines or steam-powered bicycles or glowing trees or mechanical badgers puttering across the grounds. And the house itself was just sitting there. It wasn't rolling or floating or flying or digging or spinning in the air. It was just acting like a normal house.

In fact, the only odd thing I noticed was how normal everything seemed. We walked into the Baron Estate, and we saw that M was in the living room sweeping the floor. I could hear Aunt Dorcas and Rose Blackwood in the kitchen, practicing their baking for the upcoming Pitchfork Fair. I was really looking forward to that fair.

They always served lots of pie, cake, donuts, cookies, and ice cream at the fair. I would literally go *anywhere* in the world if they were serving pie, cake, donuts, cookies, and ice cream there.

"Hello, W.B.," M said, setting her broom aside. "Who is your friend?"

"This is B.W.," I told her. "He's new."

"It's a pleasure to meet you, Mrs. Baron," B.W. said politely as he shook my mother's hand. "Your son has told me a lot about you and your husband. I like to consider myself a bit of an inventor too. I'd love it if you could show me some of your fantastic inventions one day."

This pleased my mother, who promised B.W. that she would be more than happy to show him some of her and my father's inventions.

"Speaking of your father," M said, turning to me with a smile, "he's out back, W.B. And he's got a little surprise to show you."

". . . Oh."

I've heard that some children get excited when they hear that one of their parents has a surprise to show them. I am not one of those children. For most children, a surprise from your father might mean a new bicycle or a deck of cards or a trip to the ocean. But for me, it was usually something weird and confusing, like a strange new invention that would transform my fingers into sausages, or something like that. At the very best, I could expect to be given a new hat.

My father has a strange thing about hats. He takes them very seriously. *Very* seriously.

With B.W. following close behind, I walked through the house and out the back door, where I spotted my father and someone who I hadn't been expecting to see.

"Hi there, W.B.!" my father chirped happily, as he gently petted his new friend.

His new friend was a brown Arabian horse with a shaggy, black mane. I could tell by the way my father was looking at it that the horse had instantly become his new favorite member of the family. My father loves animals. In fact, I'm pretty certain that he loves them more than he loves people. People confuse him, and he confuses people. Animals he understands, and, for some reason, animals understand him as well. Maybe he was just born the wrong species.

"Hey there!" another familiar voice cried.

I couldn't see the person who cried out because she was standing behind Aunt Dorcas's butter churner. But even if I hadn't recognized her voice, there was only one person I knew who was short enough to be blocked by a butter churner.

It was my old friend from Chicago. Her name was Iris, but everyone called her Shorty. They called her that because she was half the size of most kids our age. In fact, there were infants who could stand up and look at her, eye-to-eye. But you couldn't let her size fool you. Shorty was, by far, the strongest and toughest kid I'd ever met. As she sped across the yard and jumped up into my arms, she gave me a hug so powerful that, for a moment, my eyes bulged out of my head, my chest caved in, and my mouth made an involuntary ERRRRNNNTTT! noise.

"ERRRRNNNTTT!"

Shorty was dressed in her usual western style: a work shirt and vest, with a little cowboy hat perched on top of her head.

"How's it going, W.B.?" she cried before giving me a playful punch on the arm, which knocked me over. "I see you're still as graceful as a one-legged hog in a flooded pigpen."

I picked myself up and cleaned the mud out of my ear before I patted her on the shoulder.

"It's great to see you too, Shorty," I said. "What are you doing here? Why aren't you in Chicago?"

"His name is Geoffrey," my father said, as he continued to gently stroke the horse's mane. "He's the newest member of our family. Isn't he a good horse?"

"I'm here because of Pa," Shorty told me. "There was a terrible fight in his tavern, and someone ripped half his mustache from his face. It tore up his lip something fierce, but he was more upset about the mustache. The taxidermist had charged him six dollars for it."

Shorty's father runs a tavern back in Chicago. He's . . . what you might call a *strange* sort of person. He was unable to grow a proper mustache, but, since he'd always wanted a mustache, he started gluing animal tails to his upper lip to make it look as though he had one. He started off using rabbit tails, but then, when other men started growing bigger and bushier mustaches, he switched to squirrel tails, then raccoon tails, and finally beaver tails.

Like I said, he was a very strange person.

"Ouch," I said, rubbing my upper lip in sympathy.

"Yeah. But there's a special doctor here in Arizona Territory who should be able to help him. We read about him in a fancy magazine back in Chicago. This special doctor, who is also a barber, and who also sells used shoes on the weekend, is known for brewing some sort of miracle oil that will grow hair on your upper lip."

"Really?"

"Geoffrey has very intelligent eyes," P said as he considered his horse's eyes. "You can tell how intelligent a horse is by his eyes."

"Yup," Shorty told me with a nod, ignoring my father. "The doctor said that if Pa dabs a little bit of the miracle oil on his upper lip every day for six weeks, he should end up with a mustache thicker than my Great Aunt Megan's, which is pretty darn thick. So, we'll be in town for the next few weeks while the doctor sews up Pa's lip, and then gives him a few doses of the miracle oil. Say, who's your friend?"

For a moment, I was confused by what she meant, but then I remembered I had brought a friend home with me from school—a friend who was still standing quietly behind me. B.W. had been waiting politely, listening to

Shorty's strange story about her strange father while stealing glances at my equally strange father, who had taken out his sewing kit and was beginning to sew his new horse a hat.

"Horses love hats," P told us. "Few people know this. But it's true."

"My name is Belford Eustace Nigel Egbert Doolittle Ignatius Cattermole Threepwood Whitestone the Third," B.W. said as he stepped forward to shake Shorty's hand. "But everyone calls me B.W. I'm—aaaaahhhhhhh!"

I forgot to warn B.W. that Shorty has one of the strongest grips in the world. Shaking hands with her can feel like shaking hands with an angry gorilla. She once gave me a neck rub when I was stressed, and, afterwards, I couldn't feel my legs for six days.

"It's a pleasure to meet you, B.W.," Shorty said with a grin. "My name's Iris, but everyone with a working pair of eyeballs calls me Shorty. Glad to see old Wide Butt here finally found himself another pardner."

Ahem.

I should point out that "Wide Butt" is *not* a real nickname of mine. Shorty was just joking. That's all. Pretend you didn't just read that. Pretend you read something else instead. Hey, did you know that in 1848, Niagara Falls stopped flowing for over a day because the Niagara River was blocked up by ice? Isn't that an interesting fact? Think about that instead. Niagara Falls.

Shorty gave B.W. a friendly pat on the shoulder, and, when B.W. had picked himself up off the ground, he forced himself to offer her a smile.

"It's nice to meet you too, Shorty," he said, as he alternated rubbing his aching shoulder and his throbbing hand. "That's . . . that's a mighty firm handshake you have. Oh my gosh, I can't feel my fingertips . . ."

"Should I sew a feather onto Geoffrey's hat?" P asked us. "Oh, never mind. That's a silly question. *Of course* I'll sew a feather onto his hat."

Finally, my curiosity got the best of me.

"When did you decide to buy a horse?" I asked P.

"He didn't buy it," Shorty said proudly. "I brought Geoffrey here as a thank-you gift. Your pa was kind enough to give me your old horse, Magnus, after I helped you defeat Benedict Blackwood, so I wanted to return the favor. I've won several cattle roping and trick riding contests lately, and they keep giving me horses as prizes. This here was one of my favorite horses. He's smarter than a whip and twice as quick. I knew that your dad would like him."

"I think I'll give him *two* feathers in his cap," P said as he continued to work on his new horse's hat.

Shorty turned to B.W., who I noticed was slowly backing away from us. He had the look on his face that most people got when they realized how weird my family is. And he hadn't even seen anything particularly weird yet. That wasn't a good sign.

"Mrs. Baron invited me to stay for supper," she said to my new friend. "I hope you're staying too, B.W. I heard that W.B.'s Aunt Dorcas is cooking a chicken pot pie, which is my absolute favorite."

It was my favorite too. Actually, *all* food was my favorite, except for spinach, which I don't really count as food. I think of it more as a soggy stinkweed that people make their children eat because they secretly hate them.

"Oh, I'm sorry, but I don't think I can stay," B.W. said slowly.

My father finally looked up from his new favorite family member.

"We'd love to have you over for supper, B.W.," said P. "I heard you tell my wife that you're interested in inventions. We have quite a few inventions around here that might tickle your brain."

"*Tickle his brain?* Is that a good thing?" I asked.

I hated having my armpits and feet tickled, so I could only imagine how uncomfortable it must be to have your brain tickled. It would probably make you feel as though you'd just had a really big idea. Or like your brain had to sneeze. Either way, I didn't think I'd like it. I have enough terrible ideas without my brain being tickled.

"Wait a minute," said B.W. with a frown. "How did you know that I told Mrs. Baron about my interest in inventions? You couldn't possibly have heard that from all the way out here."

My father reached into his ear and produced a tiny mechanical device that looked a bit like a snail that was made of metal. It had a single, blinking red light in the middle of it.

"This is one of my favorite inventions," he told us. "I call it the *Listen Up, Stephen!* Device. When I place it in my ear, I can hear everything that's going on within 500 feet of me. And I mean *everything*."

He placed the *Listen Up, Stephen!* Device back in his ear and listened.

"Right now, I can hear that my wife is busy fixing the ice box, Rose Blackwood is telling Aunt

Dorcas not to cry in her pie filling, there is a lizard scuttling across our front steps, a family of squirrels is climbing a tree behind the garden shed, two crows down the road are having an argument, and W.B.'s stomach is about to rumble quite loudly."

My stomach then rumbled quite loudly.

I had to admit, it was a pretty good invention.

"That's brilliant," B.W. said, his eyes growing wider than wagon wheels. "It's an absolutely incredible invention, Mr. Baron. But why do you call it the *Listen Up, Stephen!* Device?"

"Great question," my father replied with a cheery smile. "I call it that because the invention helps you to listen."

"But why *Stephen?*"

"Why *not* Stephen?" P answered.

That's what you get for asking my father a silly question. You get another silly question in return.

"Huh," B.W. said with a frown. "Okay. Well, I have to go home now, sir. Otherwise my family might get worried. I'd love to come over for supper another day though, if you'll allow me to. And perhaps show me some more of your *interesting* inventions? I bet you make blueprints for all your inventions, don't you? So that you'll know how to build them again, in case something happens to them?"

"Of course we do," said P. "And we'd love to have you over. The more the merrier. Hmmmmm. Maybe I should add some sparkles and sequins to the hat as well . . ."

B.W. shook my hand and told me that he'd see me tomorrow at school before he quickly jogged around the side of the house and started his journey on the path leading back to Downtown Pitchfork. Shorty and I watched my new friend disappear over the large sandy lumps of the desert as the sun slowly began to fall. B.W. certainly seemed in quite a hurry to get home. I hoped that I hadn't gotten him into trouble with his family.

"That was a little strange," Shorty said to me.

"I know," I said. "Why would a horse want sequins on its hat?"

A Very Familiar Shoe

As we made our way inside to wash up and set the table for supper, Shorty explained to me that it wasn't Geoffrey the horse's hat that she had found strange. It was B.W.

"What do you mean?" I asked. "There's nothing strange about him. He's a perfectly normal kid. Considering how weird my family is, I think he acted just fine."

Shorty shrugged as she stood on a stepstool to reach the kitchen sink.

"Maybe you're right," she said. "I just got a weird sort of feeling from that kid, that's all. There's something I can't quite put my finger on that's bothering me about him . . ."

I handed her a towel as I rolled my eyes. B.W. was a perfectly normal and nice kid. It was clear to me that

Shorty was just being paranoid. And maybe a bit jealous too. After all, before B.W. came around, she was my only friend. Now she had a bit of competition.

"Well, you're the only one who got a weird feeling from him," I told her as we walked to the dining room. "Everyone else likes him a lot. You'd like him too if you spent more time with him."

"Maybe," Shorty agreed as she stacked three books onto one of the dining room chairs before hopping onto them and sitting down. "But right now, the only thing I'd like to spend more time with is that chicken pot pie."

I agreed with her. The smells coming from the dinner table were so good that my mouth had started to water like a leaky faucet. In my life, I've flown thousands of feet over the ground in a flying machine and stood at the bottom of the sea in an underwater breathing suit, and I can tell you with certainty that if there's anything more beautiful in this world than a full supper table, I've yet to see it.

I should mention that I'm really quite fond of food. It is my favorite thing.

"Where's B.W.?" M asked, sitting beside me at the table. "Didn't you let him know that he was invited for supper? I was just telling Rose that you had finally made a friend at school."

"I wanted to see him for myself," Rose commented as she began to cut slices of the chicken pot pie for everyone. "I needed to know if he was real or just imaginary."

"Ha ha ha," I said dryly, rolling my eyes. "You're hilarious. You ought to be on the stage. People pay good money for funny things like you."

Shorty giggled as she accepted a large slice of pot pie from Rose.

"I thought it was pretty funny," Shorty told me, and then she playfully pinched my leg from under the table, causing me to yelp.

I've had the black and blue bruise from Shorty's playful pinch for over a month and a half now, and I'm beginning to wonder if it'll ever go away.

The next morning at school, I sat there with the rest of the class and watched as B.W. struggled through his first oral report. Miss Danielle loved assigning us reports to present to the class. In fact, sometimes it felt like all we did at school was either give reports or listen to the other kids give reports. The kids at my school might not be strong readers, and we might need to use our fingers and toes to do arithmetic, and the only real science we'd ever been taught was that frogs and toads weren't the same thing (though Miss Danielle had never explained to us the actual difference between them), but we're pretty darn good at talking for long periods of time about things that we don't really know or care about.

"Ummm . . ." he began, nervously adjusting his collar and combing his hair back with his fingers. "My name is B.W."

"No, it isn't!" Miss Danielle called from her desk at the other end of the room. "Your name is Belford Eustace Nigel Egbert Doolittle Ignatius Cattermole Threepwood Whitestone the Third! I've been practicing, so now I can say it quite quickly, over and over again. Would you like to hear?"

Miss Danielle did not allow us to use nicknames in class, which was why she always called me Waldo instead of W.B. When there were two students in class who had the same first name, instead of allowing one of them to shorten their name, she would refer to them by both their first and last names. When two students in class happened to have the same first and last name, she would refer to them by their first name and last name, followed by a very brief description of them. That explained why the two Christopher Crons in my class were known as "Christopher Cron with the Runny Nose" and "Christopher Cron with the Normal Nose."

"That's alright," B.W. said quickly, before Miss Danielle could start repeating his name. "I'm sure you're quite good at saying it fast. Anyway, my family moved here last week. And now we live in a little house in—"

"I'm sorry to interrupt!" Miss Danielle interrupted in a way that didn't sound particularly sorry. "But you moved here from *where*?"

The other kids in class turned and began to whisper to their friends. Unfortunately, the only friend I had who I could whisper to was currently standing in front of the class. I tried to whisper to him loudly, so he could hear me.

Apparently, "whispering loudly" is also known as "simply talking," which is not allowed when a student is giving a report in front of the class. So I was forced to listen to the rest of my friend's report while sitting in the corner with the dunce cap on my head. Which was alright. My head was getting a bit cold anyway.

"I . . . uh . . ." B.W. stammered as he glanced at the map of the world that was tacked to our wall. "I moved here from . . . from . . . Greece?"

"Greece?" Miss Danielle exclaimed in a shocked tone. "Goodness! That's very far away. Do you speak Greek?"

"They speak *Greek* in Greece?" said Christopher Cron with the Runny Nose. "Wow. And they're actually able to understand each other?"

"Uh, I don't know," B.W. said quickly. "I'm actually not from *that* Greece. I mean, I'm from Greece, New York. Yeah, that's right. It's a small town in upstate New York. You probably wouldn't have heard of it. It's not on any maps."

"How do you find your way around if it isn't on a map?" one student asked.

"And how do you know that you're actually there?" Christopher Cron with the Normal Nose added.

"You just do," B.W. told them. "I moved to Pitchfork from Greece, New York, and now I live here with my father."

"What does your father do?" Miss Danielle asked.

B.W. paused for a moment. I could tell by the pause that he was uncomfortable discussing his family. I could understand that. Usually, when I discussed my family, I got into trouble and ended up where I was at that moment— in the corner of the classroom with my favorite pointy cap on top of my head. I wondered if the same thing would happen to B.W. If so, Miss Danielle would have to buy a second dunce cap, because I didn't really want to share. The dunce cap likely wasn't large enough to fit both of our heads.

"He works for a bank," B.W. finally said. "My grandparents used to work for banks too, but they're retired. I really like science, and horses, and collecting coins. My old school was very different than this one. It was bigger, and we never had to give oral reports to the class. But I still like it here in Pitchfork. I hope my family can stay here for a long time. Thank you. I'm finished with my report, Miss Danielle."

Miss Danielle glanced up at the clock mounted on the schoolhouse wall.

"The clock says you still have twenty-two and a half minutes left," she told him.

"But I've run out of things to say."

"That doesn't matter," Miss Danielle said. "I assigned a thirty-minute report, and I expect you to give a thirty-minute report. So keep reporting."

But B.W. had nothing else to say. He continued to stand there in front of the class, and the kids continued to whisper to one another, and Miss Danielle continued to sit behind her desk, and I continued to adjust my dunce cap, until the twenty-two and a half minutes finally passed, and my friend could take his seat again.

Shorty and her parents were staying at a hotel in Downtown Pitchfork while her father received treatment from the brilliant doctor/barber/weekend-used-shoe-salesman, but she spent a lot of time with us at the Baron Estate. I liked having her around. Rose Blackwood joked that she was my girlfriend, but I didn't care. Shorty was teaching me how to properly jump a horse, which I'd always wanted to learn to do.

With my father's permission, Shorty saddled and mounted Geoffrey and galloped to the far end of our property. Then, with a whip of the reins and a little shout, she rode Geoffrey as quickly as she could across our backyard, and when she reached the little white picket fence that surrounded the Baron Estate, she pulled up on the horse's reins, signaling it to jump. Geoffrey's jump was quite graceful, and, when he landed, he spun around to face me and took a little bow. Shorty hopped off the saddle and gave a short curtsy as well.

I couldn't help but applaud. She was a mighty fine jumper.

It didn't go quite so smoothly when I tried it.

First, I accidentally hopped onto the saddle backwards, so I was facing Geoffrey's tail instead of his head. When I tried to jump off so I could correct my positioning, my foot got caught in the horse's reins. Geoffrey felt the pull and thought I was directing him to gallop, so he began to gallop.

Since I was facing backwards, and had nothing to hold on to, I did the only thing I could think of.

I panicked and started to scream.

But I did it in a very brave and manly way.

At least, that's what Shorty told me later when I asked her how I looked.

As I screamed, I flailed my arms around, which probably wasn't such a great idea because I lost my balance and fell off the horse. But since my foot was still tangled in the reins, I was dragged all the way across the rocky yard surrounding our property, kicking up a cloud of dust so thick that it looked like London fog. While I was being dragged, I tried to grab onto anything I could, but the large rocks and little saplings that I caught ahold of just ripped out of the ground.

When we finally reached the fence, I screamed at Geoffrey, "DON'T JUMP!", but since I was choking on dust and my mouth was filled with rocks and cacti, it must have sounded like I screamed, "GO JUMP!" because that is exactly what he did.

Geoffrey cleared the fence without trouble, soaring through the sky with admirable grace. But I wasn't so lucky. As Geoffrey completed his graceful jump by landing gently on the ground like he did before, my face smacked right into the fence, breaking it apart.

And by "it," I mean the fence. Not my face. Though considering how I'd be the one who'd have to fix the broken fence, I sort of wish that it was my face that'd been broken instead. I wouldn't be expected to spend all day Sunday rebuilding and repainting my face.

When the world stopped spinning, and the little laughing squirrels stopped dancing around my head (when I'm dizzy or confused, I see squirrels . . . I don't know why, so don't ask), I slowly stood up and pulled my boot from the horse's reins. I looked over and saw Shorty staring at me in astonishment.

"Wow, W.B.," she finally said, when the power of speech returned to her. "That's the most incredible jump that I've ever seen."

That's probably the nicest thing she could have said after seeing me display such a remarkable lack of riding talent, coordination, common sense, and . . . well . . . a lack of just about everything that a person could be lacking.

Isn't she a great friend?

When Shorty wasn't staying at the Baron Estate, B.W. was usually there. It was great always having a friend over, even though at times it seemed like B.W. only came over to talk to my parents and learn about their inventions and devices.

"Can you tell me more about the material you've invented that's both bulletproof and fireproof?" he asked as he sat with my father at his work bench. "That sounds fascinating to me. How do you make it? And why is it so lightweight?"

As my father started to give a very long, very detailed, and very boring explanation about the science behind his seemingly impossible invention, I sat in the corner and listened to the ridiculous music that played in my head.

"*Doo dee doo dee dooo duhhhh*," I sang quietly, as my brain started coming up with strange questions to distract me from their conversation, like if fish ever get cold in the water, and what the purpose of ear hair is . . . when suddenly I heard something strange.

I stopped singing as the wacky music in my mind shut off in an instant. My father was still giving his long explanation to B.W., who had pulled out a little notepad so he could write down P's answer. I stood up, and walked over to the open window at the back of the work garage.

I couldn't be one hundred percent certain, but I thought I had heard the very distinct sound of someone sneezing outside. The sneeze was followed by a frantic rustling noise, which sounded very much like a person who'd been hiding in the bushes, who suddenly realized that their sneeze had given away their hiding place, and now they were quickly trying to escape without being seen.

At least, that's what it sounded like to me.

I suppose the reason why that unimportant little sound caught my attention was because over the past couple of days, I'd been getting the strangest feeling. It felt as though someone was *watching* me. Sometimes I got that feeling while I was lying in bed at night, preparing to go to sleep. Sometimes I got that feeling while I was sitting down at the table to enjoy my second or eighth lunch of the day. And sometimes, I got the feeling when I was walking to school in the morning, crossing the Pitchfork Desert just as the sun was rising. Of course, I never *saw* anyone watching me, but that didn't make the feeling go away. I had yet to tell anyone about the feeling, because I was worried they would think there was something wrong with my brain. My parents often worried about the state of my brain. If you'd injured your head as often as I have, people would be worrying about the state of your brain too.

I stuck my head out of the garage window and looked outside. The bushes certainly looked as though someone had been hiding in them. For one thing, they were almost completely crushed, which was a pretty good sign that someone was in them. The animals that made temporary homes in our bushes were usually much neater and much more careful, and they weren't heavy enough to leave behind such large footprints.

And for another thing, someone had accidentally left their shoe behind.

It was a very familiar shoe.

PRETTY SQUIRRELS . . .

I'm no detective. I'm barely even a . . . whatever-it-is that I am.

I've read plenty of mystery books about brilliant inspectors who can spot a snapped twig or a spilled bit of soup, and from that little piece of evidence they can use their brilliant detective brains to solve a crime. My brain isn't that clever. In fact, my brain often won't tell me where I left my pants the previous evening.

But even I could recognize one of Rose Blackwood's shoes when I saw it. For one thing, she was the only person I knew who wore bright red cowboy boots that had "*R.B.*" printed on them in cursive lettering.

I leaned out of the window and picked up the boot. After telling P and B.W. that I would be right back, I left the work garage and went back into the house.

My father and B.W. probably didn't even notice that I had left.

I found Rose Blackwood in the kitchen with Aunt Dorcas. They'd been spending a lot of time working together, preparing pies and cakes and tarts to enter into the Pitchfork Fair baking contest. The Pitchfork Fair's baking contest was a big deal, and it was taken *very* seriously by everyone in town. You might say that they took it a bit *too* seriously. Many terrible fights had broken out over what someone considered to be a misjudged pie or tart. There were families in town that had been feuding for decades over a single nasty comment made about the heavy-handed use of raisins or a sad lack of cinnamon in a dessert. Miss Danielle's mother had once gone nine months without speaking to anyone in town after her famous blueberry pie had come in second place. A judge was once shot in the knee with a crossbow when he dared to suggest that a contestant's strawberry cake was a little too dry. The judge's grandmother later apologized to him for the shooting and told him that she had simply lost her temper.

Aunt Dorcas was a wonderful cook and an excellent baker. Rose Blackwood was a pretty good cook, but her baking was . . . well . . . I suppose you could compare her baking to my horseback riding, only not quite as good.

"Oh my," said Aunt Dorcas with a sickly expression as she pulled Rose's latest cake creation out of the oven. "What on earth happened to this chocolate cake?"

I could see what she meant. I'd never seen a chocolate cake that was green before. It was sort of shaped like a fish too, and not a particularly healthy-looking fish either. But the worst part about the cake wasn't the way it looked. It was the way it smelled. It smelled like a combination of burning rubber and rotten cabbage. My eyes began to water from all the way across the room.

"Did you mean to shape the cake like a depressed trout?" Aunt Dorcas asked Rose Blackwood.

"Umm, yes?"

"Well, next time, don't do that. Most people do not like

to think of melancholy seafood when they're eating dessert."

Rose grumbled to herself as she dumped her fish cake into the garbage. It wasn't the first fishy cake she'd dumped that day, and I doubted it would be the last.

"Rose?" I said.

Rose continued to grumble as she pulled another one of her terrible cakes from the oven.

The second cake looked like a squished toad, but the shape of the cake wasn't even the strangest thing about it. The color was positively bizarre. It was *silver*. How she could turn a butter cream cake silver is still baffling to me. It seemed impossible. But then again, a lot of the things that happened to my family seemed pretty impossible. Maybe we're just lucky. Or in the case of my unbelievable clumsiness and Rose's consistently foul cakes, maybe we're a bit cursed as well.

"I think this is yours, Rose!" I called out in a loud voice. "Were you just outside? Behind the work garage? Lying in the bushes? Sneezing with only one boot on?"

I held up the red cowboy boot. Rose finally looked at me.

"Oh," she said, looking a bit embarrassed. "I've been looking for that. Thank you, W.B. No, I've been in here baking all day. Please just leave my boot there in the corner. I'll put it in my bedroom once I'm finished with my pies."

Aunt Dorcas picked up one of the pies that Rose had baked. She sniffed it, and her face turned the same sickly shade as Rose's fishy chocolate cake.

"Are you sure you aren't already finished in here?" my aunt asked hopefully. "Maybe what you need is a nice break from the kitchen."

"No," Rose insisted, "I want to keep trying until I get it right."

Aunt Dorcas frowned as she quietly dumped the stinky pie into the trashcan, on top of all the other failed desserts that Rose had attempted to bake that day. The kitchen was beginning to smell a bit like an overflowing pig trough in the middle of August.

While Rose Blackwood continued to mix ingredients into her mixing bowl, muttering to herself about how this was bound to be her first tasty cake or pie, I looked at her sleeves and her pants. They were covered in dark stains, though I couldn't be certain if the stains were chocolate or dirt.

It was the day of the Pitchfork Fair, a day that I'd been looking forward to since the last fair ended, exactly one year earlier. Fair day was my absolute favorite day of the year. I would gladly give up my birthday for the next ten years if it meant that the Pitchfork Fair happened twice a year instead of only once. I was so excited about all the delicious foods they would be serving at the fair that I didn't eat anything the day before, so I would have plenty of room in my stomach.

Well, I did eat a *little* bit. After all, it's not a good idea to starve yourself. But aside from a few hot dogs, cheese sandwiches, a few slices of chocolate cake, toast, eggs, bacon, fried chicken, turkey, ham, sausage, apples, and about two dozen bananas . . . I really didn't eat much of anything the day before the fair.

I had invited both B.W. and Shorty to come with me, and they had both sounded quite excited about it.

Until they learned that the other might be coming as well.

"Really?" B.W. had said to me in school, when I told him that Shorty would most likely be joining us. "You really want that tiny girl to come along too?"

"Yes. Why not? I like Shorty. She's a lot of fun."

B.W. shrugged as he sat down at his desk, and I sat

down at mine. Well, I *attempted* to sit at my desk, but I missed my chair and fell, somehow poking myself in the eye with my ankle.

I'm genuinely starting to wonder if maybe I am cursed. It wouldn't be the first time . . .

"I suppose she is fun," B.W. began as he pulled out his homework. "Sort of. But I guess that my problem with her is that she's, well, don't you think she's a little bit . . . immature?"

"Huh?"

Immature? Shorty? I mean, I guess she could be a bit silly at times, and she had a habit of giving people unflattering nicknames, like when she'd call me Wide B—whatever that nickname was that she called me earlier which now I can't remember. *Ahem.* But did I actually consider her to be *immature*?

"Maybe a little bit," I said. "But she's still a nice person."

"Of course she's a nice person," B.W. said as he smiled at me. "She's a very nice person. I'm the first one who'd say that about her. But hanging out with her is sort of like hanging out with a little kid. And I don't really want to hang out with a little kid, do you?"

Shorty's opinion of B.W. was no better. In fact, it was about twelve and a half times worse.

"He's a creep," she said, when I mentioned that he would be going to the fair with us.

"Tell me what you honestly think about him."

"I think he's a slimy creep."

"But how do you *really* feel?"

"He's a slimy, creepy fool who is clearly hiding something from you," Shorty said quite plainly.

"Shorty, if you have an opinion on him, *please* be upfront with me about it. Stop speaking in vague riddles."

"He's a slimy, creepy, foolish hider who shouldn't be trusted by you or by your parents."

"Well, if you can't give me a straight answer, then I'll just stop asking you."

"Stop kidding around, W.B.," Shorty said as she shoved me. "Look, I'm glad you're starting to make friends here in Pitchfork, but I don't think B.W. is who you think he is. There's something really fishy about that kid, and I don't like it."

As I climbed back into the house (Shorty had managed to knock me across the room and out the window with a single shove), I noticed something a bit fishy too. But it wasn't B.W. It was yet another terrible odor coming from the kitchen. This one was even worse than usual.

"Excuse me," I said to Shorty as I made my way to the kitchen to see what was happening.

As I opened the door to the kitchen, I was knocked back by a powerful stench that hit me in the nose like a stinky fist.

"Oh goodness!" I cried, as I immediately buried my nose in my hands.

I gagged. The smell was so bad that it attacked every sense that I had, including my sense of sight, my sense of hearing, and my sense of touch. The stink burned my eyes and my skin, and it left a smelly ringing sound in my ear. How can a smell make a ringing sound, you ask? Well, that's a darn good question. Congratulations. You're a good question asker. The answer is: I don't know, but I know that it did, and it was absolutely awful.

The smell was so bad that I dropped to the floor and groaned, completely overwhelmed by an odor so terrible that I feared it would live in my nostrils forever. It was so bad that it paralyzed me. I couldn't move. I couldn't breathe. It was like I'd been kicked in the breadbasket by an ornery mule. My life passed before my eyes for the second time, and it included the first time that my life had passed before my eyes a few months ago, which made the whole thing take a really long time. I was about to die from exposure to that horrible odor. They'd have to bury my body in the middle of the desert so it wouldn't stink up the cemetery.

Suddenly, I felt someone grab me by the hair and pull me out of the kitchen and into the safety of the living room. As the kitchen door slammed shut behind me, I felt my body begin to return to normal again.

"Wheeew!" Shorty said, her little eyes beet red and watering. "That's something foul in there! I reckon it smells like someone left two tons of rotten onions in the sun, and then tried to cover up the stink with a carriage full of rancid milk and fresh cow plop!"

"It's much worse than that," I gasped, pulling out my handkerchief to wipe my sweaty face. "It smells like someone turned that kitchen into an outhouse for all of Arizona Territory. My eyes are running so badly from the smell that they're trying to jump off my face and dash out the door!"

Shorty giggled as she helped me open the windows in the living room to air out the Baron Estate.

"It smells like a bunch of dead octopuses that someone covered in sweaty stockings, and then—"

"Alright, I get it!" a very cross-sounding voice interrupted. "I know it smells bad in there. I don't need to hear your sass-mouthed jokes and frumps about it."

Shorty and I turned around and saw a very angry and very hurt looking Rose Blackwood. She was dressed in one of Aunt Dorcas's aprons, with her hair and clothing covered in flour, sugar, syrup, and burnt splotches of berries and chocolate. She smelled nearly as gross as one of her pies.

"Sorry," Shorty and I said as we tried to hold in our giggles.

"It was supposed to be a cherry pie," Rose said as she opened another window, picked up a blanket, and tried to fan the stink out of the house. "But then something went horribly wrong, and it started to look more like a cake. So I added some chocolate and tried to make it a cherry chocolate cake. But then something went really horribly wrong, and it started to look more like a pudding. So I added some vanilla to it and tried to make it a cherry, chocolate, and vanilla pudding. But then something went really, really, horribly wrong, and it started to look like candy. So I added some nuts and tried to make it cherry, chocolate, vanilla, and nut candy. And then something went really, really, really, horribly, awfully wrong, and it turned into . . ."

"Cow plop?" Shorty suggested.

"Shorty, go home," Rose said darkly.

"Okay!" Shorty said brightly. "I'll see you at the fair tomorrow, W.B. Hopefully I won't be seeing Belford Eustace Nigel Egbert Doolittle Ignatius Cattermole Threepwood Whitestone the Third there too."

She skipped out of the house and closed the door behind her. When she was gone, Rose turned to me with a quizzical look on her face.

"Who is Belmont Useless Eggsnerd No-neck Threestone . . . whatever it is she said?"

"B.W."

"Oh," Rose said, as she wiped some of the burnt chocolate from her eyebrows. "I like that kid. He's much politer than your bouncy little friend."

"They don't like each other very much. In fact, I think B.W. and Shorty actually hate each other. And I don't understand why. I don't know what to do about it. Do you? Maybe I should have—"

"Not now, W.B.," Rose said, already making her way back to the kitchen. "I have less than twenty-four hours to make a decent dessert for the Pitchfork Fair baking contest. Do me a favor and stay out of the kitchen. And please don't bother me. This is very important."

That night, I was once again struck with the terrible, annoying, frightening, and all-too-familiar feeling that someone was watching me. I was lying in bed and slowly drifting off to sleep, when suddenly the feeling hit me like a runaway donkey cart.

It was an awful feeling, like someone had just doused me with a barrel full of ice water. I actually felt someone's eyeballs on me. But not just any eyeballs. These were *angry* eyeballs. The sort of eyeballs that would jump out of their owner's face and blink you to death if they could. It was a very unsettling feeling.

But not nearly as unsettling as what happened next.

Without moving an inch, I slowly opened one eye and peeked towards my bedroom window.

From the light of the moon, I could see the shadow of a very tall and very dangerous-looking person. They were peering into my bedroom and watching me.

I'm not what you would call *fast* or *quick* or even *average* when it comes to moving. In fact, I'm what some of you might call *lazy* or *lethargic* or *slower than a depressed slug*. But in that instant, I became quicker than lightning. I jumped out of bed and crossed my room in two long strides, threw open the door, dashed down the hallway, and then fell down the long staircase of the Baron Estate in less than three seconds flat.

As I lay there on the bottom step, the giant lump already forming on the back of my skull, I smiled at the pink and purple squirrels which danced around my head as I slowly lost consciousness.

"Pretty squirrels . . ." I mumbled. "Such pretty squirrels . . ."

BLINDED BY THE SPRAY OF HOT PEAR FILLING

"W.B.? Are you alright? Can you hear me?"

They were talking to me. How nice. My eyes fluttered. My vision was blurred, so all I could see was the outline of the three large squirrels standing over me. One of them was gently dabbing my forehead with a wet washcloth, which I thought was really sweet. I figured that I should be nice to the squirrels in return and promise to give them acorns and talk to them about squirrel things.

"Hello, squirrels," I murmured through lips that felt as though they were made of molasses. "Find any good nuts lately?"

"Oh dear, do you think he's suffered brain damage?"

"No. I'm afraid that's just what he's like when he's

waking up. W.B.! You were having another strange dream!"

Someone splashed a glass of cold water in my face. I sputtered and sneezed, then wiped my face and rubbed my eyelids. When I opened my eyes, instead of three giant squirrels, I saw M, P, and Aunt Dorcas standing over me. Which I suppose made a lot more sense.

"Oh," I said as I slowly tried to sit up. "Hello, everyone."

"Are you alright, W.B.?" M asked. "You must have taken a terrible tumble in the middle of the night. Why were you coming downstairs so late?"

"That's a foolish question," Aunt Dorcas said stiffly. "The boy was clearly trying to raid the ice box and eat my prized apple walnut pie and my cinnamon pear tarts before I could have the chance to enter them in the fair today."

"I was not!" I objected. "First of all, I had completely forgotten that you had a pie and tarts in the ice box!"

"If you hadn't forgotten, would you have tried to eat them?" my eggy aunt demanded.

Yes, of course I would have. But I couldn't tell her that.

"Yes, of course I would have. But I can't tell you that."

Bah. Foiled by my stupid brain again! I must have been more injured than I thought. Normally I was better at hiding things like that from Aunt Dorcas.

"If you weren't coming down for food, then why were

you sneaking downstairs in the middle of the night?" P asked.

I noticed he was sewing another hat for Geoffrey the horse. This one was more of a casual hat, with a wide brim and a big "S" sewn onto the front. My father was a strange man, but at least he was committed to his strangeness. Whenever he began a project, he saw it through to the end.

"I saw someone at my window," I explained as M helped me up. "Someone was watching me. And I think they've been watching me for a while. Lately, I've been feeling eyes on me, and they haven't been friendly eyes."

My mother frowned. Aunt Dorcas blinked. My father went back to sewing Geoffrey's hat. Before anyone could comment on what I'd said, there was a knock at the door. I limped over and answered it. It was Shorty.

"Hi, W.B.," she said sadly. "Nice pajamas."

I looked down and saw that I was wearing my white and blue polka dotted nightshirt, and a yellow nightcap with a fuzzy ball at the end. I shrugged. She was right. They were pretty nice.

"Thank you. What's wrong?"

Shorty sighed as she removed her cowboy hat and ran her tiny fingers through her curls.

"I have some bad news," she told me. "I'm not going to

be able to make it to the fair today."

I felt my heart sink.

"What? Why? We've been looking forward to going to the Pitchfork Fair for weeks. It's all we've talked about."

"I know, but my father got some really bad news yesterday," Shorty told me. "It turns out that the fancy doctor he'd been seeing in Pitchfork, the one who is also a barber and a used-shoe-salesman on the weekend . . . well, he's a con man. He's a quack. A fake. A phony. A charlatan."

"You mean he was a crook? A cheat? A grifter? A hoaxer? A swindler?" M asked.

"A humbug? A pretender? A mountebank? A flimflammer?" P asked.

"A scam artist? A fraud? A chiseler? A double-crosser? A racketeer? A pettifogger?" Aunt Dorcas asked.

"Yes to all of that," Shorty said, her lower lip beginning to tremble. "He took my father's money and ran away. And now Pa's devastated. He's getting treatment at Pitchfork Hospital for his ripped lip, which the quack sewed up wrong, and he's also getting treatment for a new rash that formed on his face from the so-called 'miracle oil' that the quack gave to him. The doctors at Pitchfork Hospital said that the miracle oil is nothing but carrot juice and camel spit. They don't know where the quack found the camel spit. There aren't even any camels in Arizona Territory!"

I pictured Shorty's father and how upset he must have been. To think that you were finally going to have your lifelong dream of growing a fantastic mustache come true, only to have that dream ripped away by a sneaky liar; it sounded horribly cruel to me. I guess it just goes to show you: never trust a doctor who sells used shoes on the weekend. You just can't trust them.

"I'm so sorry, Shorty," I said as I gave my friend a hug. "And please, tell your father that I'm sorry as well. I guess you'll want to spend some time with your folks today instead of going to the fair."

Shorty nodded as she brushed a tear from the corner of her eye.

"Yeah. Ma asked if I wouldn't mind staying with them at the hotel today, just to keep up Pa's spirits. And I can't say no to that. My poor pa is sadder than a hungry giraffe with a stiff neck. I'm sorry, W.B. I hope you have a good time today. I'll see you later."

"Wait!"

Shorty had already begun to leave, but my eggy Aunt Dorcas quickly ran to the door. In her hands, she was carrying one of her little cinnamon pear tarts. It had extra whipped cream on top, just the way that I liked it.

"Here you go, Iris," Aunt Dorcas said as she handed Shorty the tart. "I want you and your parents to have a taste of the fair, even if you can't make it there. Best of luck to you. Give your father an extra big hug from all of us."

Shorty's wide grin returned.

"Thanks, Aunt Dorcas," she said, grabbing my aunt by the waist and giving her a one-armed hug. "That's mighty sweet of you. I'll see you all soon, Barons. I hope you all have a great time at the fair. I want to hear all about it when I come back!"

And then she was gone. As my aunt tried her best to catch her breath, which Shorty had squeezed out of her as though she were a frustrated accordion player, I shuffled over and tapped Aunt Dorcas on the shoulder.

"Do you think I could get a taste of the fair for breakfast?" I asked my aunt, trying to make my eyes look as sad as possible as I gently rubbed the back of my head. "I had a terrible fall, and my head hurts really badly. Maybe I'd feel a bit better if I had a tart or two, or a few slices of your delicious apple pie? With whipped cream? Extra whipped cream maybe?"

Aunt Dorcas smiled as she placed her hand on my shoulder.

"If you touch my pie or any of my tarts, I will be forced

to bake a mincemeat pie using your fingers and toes for filling, my greedy little Waldo. Now go take a bath and get dressed. We leave for the fair in less than two hours."

My mother was still concerned about the fact that I had spotted someone staring into my bedroom window, and after I convinced her that it wasn't a dream (I reminded her that I usually only dreamed about squirrels and food), she asked my father if he had any ideas about improving the security of our home.

"Well, let's see," P told her, as he held a plate out the kitchen window and fed Geoffrey his regular breakfast of pancakes with maple syrup. "We have excellent locks on the doors, and windows which can't be picked by the pickiest lock picker. The windows are all made of an unbreakable glass, which I invented because W.B. kept crashing through them. And if an intruder tries to slide down our chimney, they'll find out the hard way that I've placed a metal grate in the middle of it, which would leave them stuck in there for good. What else should we do?"

"Maybe we can invent something that will alert us if someone is sneaking around the house at night?" M suggested. "Perhaps something that would detect anything larger than a coyote creeping around the property, which could set off a series of bells and whistles and chimes to warn us?"

"Maybe we could," P said as he scratched his head. "But what if Geoffrey wanted to peek into the house late at night? I wouldn't want an alarm to frighten him."

"You can lock him up outside. Leave him in the barn overnight. That's what most people do with their horses."

My father looked absolutely horrified by the suggestion.

There was another knock at the door. I answered it while my parents continued to discuss potential security ideas, and whether horses should be counted as family members.

"Hi W.B.," B.W. said.

"Hi B.W.," I said right back. "Want a cup of tea before we go?"

"Sure."

I let my friend inside, and, as we crossed the living room and headed for the kitchen, we spotted Rose Blackwood, who had just slipped out of her bedroom on feet that were noticeably unsteady.

"Oh dear!" she cried, as she narrowly avoided crashing into us. "I'm so sorry. I didn't see you two."

"That's alright," I answered. "We just . . . wow."

I stared at Rose Blackwood, who looked like a *completely* different person. In fact, for a moment I was so shocked by her appearance that I literally couldn't speak. I couldn't even make the sort of grunts you'd expect to hear from a person who was raised by wolves. I was shocked soundless.

Rose's lips were redder than usual. Her cheeks were pinker than usual. Her eyelids were bluer than usual. And her hair was straighter than usual. It was all very . . . unusual.

Sorry. When I'm shocked by something, I'm not good at thinking up descriptive words. In fact, I'm very . . . not good at it.

At first, I thought that Rose must have been suffering from some strange sort of tropical disease, but then I realized she had done all of that to herself *on purpose*. While I found the straightened hair and the application of face paint to be . . . unusual . . . I think what surprised me the most about Rose was what she was wearing.

She was wearing *a dress*.

Rose almost never wore dresses. In fact, the only other time I could remember seeing her wear one was several months earlier, when she had put on one of Aunt Dorcas's high collared dresses because she was pretending to be my aunt. She was pretending to be my aunt because—well, it's a really long story, a story that I've already told before, and I honestly don't have time to get into it again. Sorry, I'm just a very busy kid. You'll have to read about it some other time. Or you can just pretend that I never mentioned anything about Rose dressing up like Aunt Dorcas in the first place. That's what I usually choose to do, pretend that something never happened. It's easier that way. In fact, I'm going to pretend that I didn't say any of that to you, so I can just move on with the story.

"What happened to you?" I asked Rose, as my shocked silence finally wore off. "You look so . . . *unusual.*"

She blushed, or at least I think she blushed. It was hard to be certain with all the pink stuff that she'd smeared on her cheeks. She also smelled different. Not that Rose normally smelled bad or anything, but at that moment, she smelled unusually good, like fresh flowers mixed with fresh fruit. I don't think people were meant to smell that good. If people went around smelling that good all the time, then more animals might begin to wonder if they would enjoy the taste of human beings. It would make strolls through the countryside a lot more dangerous. That's why I always make sure to stink a little bit when I go out. Just a little, though. It's for the safety of mankind.

"I don't know what you're talking about," Rose said in a rather uncomfortable tone, as she crossed her arms over her ruffled blouse.

"Your face is different colors," I told her. "And you're wearing a brand new outfit. *A dress*. And you smell like flowers and berries. It's weird."

Rose frowned at me.

"I think she looks and smells very nice," B.W. offered.

"Thank you, B.W.," Rose said with a sniff. "It's nice to see that someone around here has good manners. I'm going to go check on the pie that I have cooling on the window-sill."

As B.W. and I continued walking to the kitchen, my friend turned to me and whispered "That's a *pie*? Heavens to Betsy, I thought someone stepped in horse plop and was drying their boot on the windowsill . . ."

M, P, Aunt Dorcas, B.W., and I climbed into our horseless carriage and prepared to leave for the Pitchfork Fair. I was so excited that I could hardly sit still. B.W. had to press on my shoulders to keep me from popping out of my seat.

"Come on, Rose!" M called. "We're going to be late!"

Rose poked her painted face out the door.

"I'll meet you all there later!" she called back. "I want to put a few finishing touches on my pie first! I'll ride Geoffrey to the fair. He looks like he wants to stretch his legs anyway."

"Alright!" P said. "Make sure he wears his afternoon hat instead of his evening hat! I wouldn't want him to look foolish!"

Rose quickly nodded her head before slamming the front door shut.

"I wonder what's going on with Rose," I whispered to B.W.

But my friend was far more interested in the horseless carriage than he was in the odd behavior of Rose Blackwood. Most people are fascinated by the horseless carriage the first time that they see it. In case you've never heard of a horseless carriage before (and I'm guessing most people haven't), let me tell you that it's exactly what it sounds like: a carriage that moves without horses. And if you want more information about it than that, then you should feel quite silly for having asked me.

"How does it work?" B.W. asked P. "What do you use

to make it go? Is it safe? Why doesn't everyone ride these things? You could make tons of them and sell them for a fortune. We'd never need horses again!"

"Don't you ever say that in front of Geoffrey," P warned. "The horseless carriage is actually quite a simple invention. You see, once you crank the handle on the front of the buggy, there is a greased, internal mechanism, which—"

And that's when the funny music started playing in my head. It played for the entire trip across the Pitchfork Desert, until we reached the fairgrounds. A few times during the scientific explanation, my mother or father would turn to me and say something, expecting me to either respond with a "huh!" or a "wow!" which I did. But every time I tried to participate in the conversation any more than that, my brain would interrupt me with a new strange question to think about, like why it's called quicksand when it seems to work slowly, or why rain will ruin a leather coat, and yet it doesn't seem to bother cows.

After what felt like an eternity, my strange thoughts and wacky music were interrupted by the real wacky music of the Pitchfork Fair. Someone in the official Pitchfork Town Band was playing an instrument that looked and sounded like the sort of thing that my father would build if P ever showed any interest in musical instruments. It was a giant piano, with long metal tubes spouting from the top where the sound came out. There were buttons located above all the piano keys, which the player punched and pulled seemingly at random. It sounded like a thousand flutes being played all at once, and it added to the excitement of the event.

The fairground was marvelously decorated, with streamers and flags and brightly colored paper lanterns. Someone kept setting off explosions of rainbow-colored confetti. There were men and women with painted faces and brightly colored clothing who were doing all sorts of strange and fantastic things like swallowing fire and juggling fish, while doing somersaults and standing on their heads. There were booths set up where local people were selling unique trinkets, fine woodwork, leatherwork, jewelry, knives, candles, and tasty homemade treats.

Miss Katherine had brought her accordion and her "circus kittens," which were really just her fifteen ordinary kittens she'd dressed up in flashy costumes; the kittens sat there and stared blankly at Miss Katherine as she danced and played the accordion. There were various tents spread throughout the grounds where inventors and magicians and salesmen were showcasing fantastic new inventions, tricks, and gadgets. Miss Danielle had a tent set up where she was offering to teach people public speaking, though people were avoiding her tent like it was covered in bees. Strangely enough, the most popular tent was the tent that actually *was* covered in bees; Mr. Dadant, the beekeeper, was giving out delicious samples of honeycomb from his buzzing little tent. Mr. Silva, the blacksmith, was showing people how to smith. Mrs. Pyramus, the weaver, was showing people how to use her giant loom to weave blankets and rugs. There was a man having an argument with a little person who was sitting on his knee—at first I thought it was a ventriloquist show, but when I sat down and watched, I discovered that it was just a man having a fight with his tiny grandmother (though it was still pretty entertaining). The Pitchfork Choir stood on a stage singing our official town anthem, which no one knew particularly well, so it involved a lot of mumbling and awkward pauses.

At the far end of the fairgrounds, there were several shooting galleries and other mounted targets where you could show off your skills with a bow and arrow, crossbow, tomahawk, throwing knife, pistol, or rifle. People seemed to be enjoying those, despite the occasional bloodcurdling scream. I guess it would be fair to say that most of the townspeople didn't have particularly good aim and would often let go of a tomahawk a bit too early. Also, I don't think it was a particularly clever idea to set up the targets in front of the line for the outhouses.

In the center of the fairgrounds, there was a long row of tables with all the delicious fair foods that I craved: cakes and candies and cookies and tarts and pies and ice cream and caramel apples and corn smothered in butter and hamburgers and sausage sandwiches and hard boiled eggs and salted peanuts and popcorn fritters and pickles and fried chicken and . . . excuse me, I appear to have drooled on myself a little bit.

While Aunt Dorcas went to the judging tables to officially enter her pie and tarts in the Pitchfork Fair baking contest, M and P immediately headed for the tents where traveling inventors were showing off their newest scientific inventions and discoveries.

"Come along, W.B. and B.W.!" M called excitedly. "We

want to tell that inventor over there, the one who invented a miniature camera, that he can get an even clearer picture if he simply uses a—"

Dooo doop bee doop baaah wooooop, the wacky music in my brain played on.

"Alright!" B.W. called to them. "We'll be right there!"

Then he turned to me.

"You don't care about the new inventions and scientific discoveries, do you?" he asked.

I shook my head no.

"You just want to go to the food tables and eat all of the sweets you can, right?"

I nodded my head yes.

"I thought so. Go ahead, W.B. I'll let your parents know where you are."

It's good to have a friend who understands you.

Two hours later, I was cut off by the three ladies who were in charge of the pie table.

"I think you've had enough," one of the ladies said.

She looked pretty nervous. I don't think she'd ever seen someone eat six pies in one sitting before, and I could tell she was worried. The other two ladies simply looked like they were in shock. One kid started applauding me as though I'd just put on a show, which I suppose I had.

"You're right," I said, as I took a bow and held in a burp. "I should probably move on to the cake table."

I slowly stood up, holding my swollen belly . . . but then I had to sit down again. I didn't feel so well. I looked in a mirror that was set up nearby and saw that my face had turned a funny shade of green. It appeared that I'd eaten myself sick. I admit that I've done that a few times before, though this was the first time I'd ever done it with pie. I didn't think it was possible. I loved pie, and pie usually loved me.

"Let me get you some water with baking soda," one of the pie ladies said, and she quickly left the food area.

"That doesn't sound very tasty!" I called to her as she disappeared into the crowd. "Maybe you could get me an ice cream instead? Or maybe some caramels?"

As I sat there with my stomach gurgling in discontent, my eyes scanned the swarm of people at the fair, some of whom I recognized, and some of whom I didn't, until finally I spotted a very familiar face that I'd been waiting to see.

"Rose!" I called, waving to my parents' assistant as I

held in another huge pie burp.

At first she didn't respond, but when I yelled her name again, she looked over at me and smiled awkwardly. She was carrying a pair of pies in her arms, and I must say that they looked much tastier than her other pies. There was nothing odd about the shape or the color. The pies also didn't have that dead fish mixed with old socks stink that the other pies had, which was good. If I'm being honest, I must say that they appeared to be perfect, like the drawings of pies you'd see in a cookbook.

"Looks like you're getting better at baking," I commented, pointing to the piping hot baked treats in her arms.

She looked at the pies and then blushed. Without saying a word to me, she moved over to the tables where the judges were busy reviewing all the entries for best cake, pie, and tart. Without looking at Rose, they collected her desserts and marked them as officially being entered in the contest. After signing her name on the official entry sheet, Rose quickly turned and left, cutting through the crowd and exiting the fairgrounds as though she was being chased by a drooling wolverine.

I was happy that she'd finally found some success at baking (after producing so many nose-crushing failures), though as I sat there rubbing my aching belly, I had to admit that there were several things that confused me.

Actually, there were hundreds of things that confused me, probably thousands, but these were the things that were confusing me at that very moment:

I was confused how Rose could bake another pair of pies so quickly, and so well. Those weren't the pies that were cooling on the windowsill. The windowsill pies had been as nasty and horrifying as all her other desserts, if not worse—one of them looked like the remains of a rotted pumpkin, and the other pie actually moaned at me, as though its filling was haunted. But the pies she placed on the judges' table looked as though they'd been baked by a professional. They looked even better than Aunt Dorcas's delicious pies.

I was also confused why Rose didn't say anything to me when I called out to her, and also why she had fled the fairgrounds so quickly. Where was she going? Was something the matter? Why would she bother entering pies into the contest if she was just going to run away before they announced the winner?

But maybe the most confusing thing to me was the fact that Rose was no longer wearing the pretty dress and the face paint. She was dressed in her regular black shirt, black pants, red cowboy boots, and her hair was once again curly and out of control. She looked like Rose again, like the Rose Blackwood we all knew and loved.

It was all very confusing.

BURP!

My parents and Aunt Dorcas sadly shook their heads at me. I suppose I was a pretty pathetic sight to see.

I was lying on one of the empty food tables with the top button of my trousers undone. The pie ladies kept bringing me water mixed with powdered rhubarb and other bitter things, with the hopes that it would soothe my sick and achy stomach.

I'm willing to admit that this was partly my fault.

"How many pies did he eat?" M asked one of the pie ladies.

"Six," one of them answered. "And then he snuck several cookies when he thought I wasn't looking."

"Only four cookies!" I protested weakly.

"And he also ate two tarts while Dr. Pearson was checking on him," another pie lady said. "And when we went to fetch him some medicine, he ate a sausage sandwich, three pieces of fried chicken, and some peanuts and popcorn."

"I needed some lunch," I explained. "I can't just eat sweets. It's not healthy."

"He also had five scoops of ice cream afterwards," the third pie lady said sourly.

"Alright, maybe that was a bit much."

"Oh, W.B.," my mother sighed. "I hope you don't get sick on the carriage ride home."

My stomach suddenly felt as though it had turned itself over and inside out. I burped into my fist and closed my eyes. For the first time in my life, the thought of food didn't sound appealing to me. I was actually full.

"I'll try not to, but I can't make you any promises, M. Say, where's B.W.?"

"He's waiting in the long line for the outhouses," Aunt Dorcas said. "I warned that boy to use the indoor bathroom back at the Baron Estate. But like you, he just didn't want to listen to reason. Why are little boys so foolish?"

"When have I ever acted foolishly?" I asked, and then I belched so loudly that a pair of old ladies standing across from me jumped and screamed.

"Ladies and gentlemen!" a loud voice cut through the air. "Please, everyone gather round! The judges of this year's cake, pie, and tart contest have decided on the winners!"

"Ooooh!" Aunt Dorcas cried. "I'm so excited! My pie and tarts are surely going to win!"

"What do you get if you win?" P asked.

"A blue ribbon!" Aunt Dorcas stated proudly.

P rolled his eyes. He reached into his pocket and pulled out a spool of blue ribbon.

"Well, if you wanted blue ribbon so badly, you should have just said something, Dorcas. I always carry some with me. How long would you like the ribbon to be?"

"Dear?" M said to P.

"Yes, my little muffin?"

"Be quiet."

"This year's official head of the Pitchfork Fair, and the man one who will announce the winners of the baking contest," the announcer continued, "is a hero to everyone who lives here in town. He needs no introduction, but I'm going to give him one anyway because he told me that I had to. Ladies and gentlemen, boys and girls, and all the rest of you too, please give a warm round of applause to our local hero, Sheriff Hoyt Opie Graham!"

Everyone broke into applause, cheering and whooping wildly for the man who they believed to be the greatest hero to ever come out of the town of Pitchfork.

I applauded too, but not quite as enthusiastically as everyone else. Sure, I liked Sheriff Graham, and I had read all the books written about his adventures. But, unlike most people, I knew that the books written about him weren't true. He wasn't a hero. In fact, he was regularly out-smarted by skunks.

But he was a very nice man who had given me my first medal, a brass medal that said "WORLD'S GREATEST GRANDMA" on it.

I'm not actually the world's greatest grandma. You see, Sheriff Graham never learned to read.

The sheriff was rumored to be retiring soon, and, from the way he looked, I'd say he was about ten years too late. He needed to be helped to the podium by a tall and skinny young man with a wild mop of red hair. Sheriff Graham was tiny and wrinkled, bald as a cue ball, and looked more like a raisin wearing a badge than a famous lawmaker. He was the sort of person you felt the need to poke every hour or so just to make sure he's still alive.

As the fairgoers continued to cheer, Sheriff Graham slowly removed his cowboy hat and waved at the crowd, revealing a fountain pen that was stuck into the top of his head.

Umm. That's my fault. You see, several months ago, I dropped a fountain pen from a great height, and it happened to land on the sheriff's head. The tip of the pen got stuck in there. A local surgeon offered to remove it, but Sheriff Graham said that he didn't want to be a bother. So, he just decided to leave the pen in his head instead. It was pretty shocking to see at first, but after a while, you just got used to it.

"Thank you," Sheriff Graham said to the crowd. "Thank you all for that kind welcome. And everyone, please, stop poking me! I'll tell you when I'm no longer alive! Anyway, I'd like to welcome you to the greatest fair in the greatest town in the greatest territory in the greatest country in the greatest world in the greatest universe of all time!"

We all cheered for that. Why not? We didn't often have things to cheer for in a town like Pitchfork, so why not cheer about our really fun fair? The skinny redheaded man who'd helped Sheriff Graham to the stage brought over a tray with three boxes on it. He held the tray up to the sheriff.

"I'd like to start by announcing the winner of the best baked tart," the sheriff continued. "But first, I need to say something to the practical joker who placed a pie tin full of goat plop on the judge's table. You might think you're funny and clever, but you're not. There's nothing funny about entering goat plop into a baking contest. For goodness' sake, I almost took a bite of it! What's funny about me ending up with a mouthful of fresh goat plop? Huh?"

Several of my classmates snickered and whispered to each other. Mr. Silva and Dr. Pearson coughed into their

fists and glanced at one another, trying their best to hide their smiles. Even I couldn't help but smirk.

I'll be the first to admit that we aren't a particularly mature town.

The sheriff cleared

his throat. "Anyway, I must say that the winner's terrific and tasty tart was by far the tastiest tart I've ever tasted in all my years of tasting terrific and tasty tarts."

Aunt Dorcas smiled brightly and patted her hair, preparing for the moment when her name would be called.

"And the winner for the best baked tart at the 1891 Annual Pitchfork Fair . . . is Miss Madge Tweetie!"

He lifted one of the boxes on the tray, revealing Miss Madge's tasty looking apple tart. Even though I was so full that I was genuinely worried I might burst, I still wouldn't have minded tasting that tart, along with a bit of whipped cream, and maybe a tall glass of mil—oh goodness, never mind.

BURP!

"Oh, how marvelous!" Madge Tweetie cried as she rushed over to the judge's table to collect her blue ribbon. "What a lovely surprise! I'm just happy that my gift of baking has finally been appreciated! I want to thank my fellow participants in the contest for giving me a good battle. And even though you're all losers, and I'm a winner, I think it's safe to say that we all had a wonderful time baking!"

Aunt Dorcas's jaw clenched so tightly that she looked in danger of crushing her teeth into powder. Madge

Tweetie was Aunt Dorcas's best friend, but she was also her worst enemy. They spent a lot of time together, and yet they seemed to hate one another with the sort of angry passion people usually directed towards poisonous spiders and deadly hurricanes. I don't understand how their friendship works, but, then again, I don't understand a lot of things about Aunt Dorcas. She didn't seem to like any of her friends, and they didn't really seem to like her either. Maybe she just doesn't know what a friend is.

I noticed that Madge had looked directly at Aunt Dorcas when she'd said the word "loser."

"If you like smooshy tarts that taste like rotten baby food, I suppose Madge's tarts are the tarts for you," Aunt Dorcas muttered to herself, before raising her voice and calling out to her best friend. "Congratulations, Madge! You absolutely deserve that! Your tart looks delicious!"

The award for best cake went to Mr. Bessie, the strange old grocer who, for some reason, always called me "Julia." He had baked what looked to be a remarkably delicious chocolate cake. He accepted the blue ribbon from Sheriff Graham and tied it around his neck like a bow tie before whooping like a loon and cakewalking out of the fairgrounds. Everyone applauded his odd exit before turning back to Sheriff Graham for the final presentation of the afternoon.

"And now," the sheriff said proudly, "the moment you've all been waiting for. I will be announcing the winner for best pie. But before I do, I'd like to thank my assistant here, who is not only my favorite employee, but also my favorite son. Ladies and gentlemen, give a big round of applause for Deputy Budford 'Buddy' Graham. Take a bow, Buddy!"

The gangly redheaded man holding the tray turned his head shyly to the crowd and blushed. The crowd politely applauded the sheriff's son, who looked more awkward than a six-thumbed grandma knitting a white sweater in a snowstorm. Someone in the crowd whistled loudly for Buddy, which made his face turn ten shades redder than his hair.

"The winner of the pie contest," Sheriff Graham continued, "has baked what I consider to be the greatest pie I've ever laid my teeth into."

I could see both Aunt Dorcas and Madge Tweetie fuss with their hair and smooth their blouses, convinced that the sheriff was about to call their name. I held in another particularly painful burp and wished that people would stop talking about pies and sweets. Didn't they realize how full I was?

"It was a delicious *pear* pie," Sheriff Graham said, and

I could see Aunt Dorcas's face crumble. "Baked by none other than . . . Miss Rose Blackwood!"

For a moment, the crowd was deadly silent. Thanks to Aunt Dorcas, stories of Rose's disgusting desserts had spread throughout Pitchfork like a rash, and absolutely no one had been expecting to hear her named the winner. But after they recovered from the shock, they broke into a very polite applause and waited for Rose to take the stage.

And then Sheriff Graham lifted the third and final box on the tray, to reveal Rose's prize winning pear pie. The moment he did, there was a tremendous explosion.

I would describe to you what happened next, but we were all blinded by a spray of hot pear filling.

MERRRRRGGGG . . .

Luckily, no one was seriously harmed from the explosion. Sheriff Graham and his son suffered a few minor injuries, but they had miraculously survived. The explosion had blown the pen right out of the top of Sheriff Graham's head, and he seemed pretty upset about that. I guess he'd just gotten used to it. It must've been pretty handy to *always* have a pen when he needed one. Personally, I'd prefer just to carry one in my pocket but to each his own.

Once I had scraped the sugar and pear slices from my eyeballs, I checked myself over and saw that I was alright too. But everyone in town was terribly frightened. The fair was immediately shut down, though we were told that we couldn't leave. The deputies in attendance all pulled out their guns as they began to investigate. The mayor of Pitchfork, Abraham Thornberry (a perfectly round man, who had been born without a neck or a sense of humor), told everyone not to worry, and to calm down, and that everything would be alright.

"But what if everything isn't alright?" Miss Katherine asked the mayor.

The mayor thought about that for a moment. "Good point. Forget what I said. Everyone panic. Panic!"

"Not so fast!" Madge Tweetie snapped. She still had a bee in her bonnet over her pie losing to Rose Blackwood's. "I think we all know what we should do next. We need to find Rose Blackwood! She's the one responsible for this! She needs to pay!"

"That's right!" Mrs. Pyramus cried. "It was her rotten pie that exploded! We should lock her up and throw away the key!"

Soon, all the townspeople of Pitchfork were angrily agreeing. They began to yell for Rose's immediate arrest, with Madge Tweetie's yell being the loudest of them all, until she discovered that there literally *was* a bee in her bonnet—one of Mr. Dadant's bees had escaped the hive and had flown into Madge's curls. Madge screamed like a sheep on fire, and dunked her head in a pig trough, while the rest of the town continued to shout about what *should* be done with Rose.

"Her brother is Benedict Blackwood! How can you trust someone who's related to the evilest villain in the world?"

"Evil runs in her blood!"

"Never trust a Blackwood! They're all no good!"

"Hey, that rhymes!"

"Take her to the jail!"

"Boot her out of town!"

"I got here late, what's going on?"

"We're turning into an angry mob!"

"Okay!"

"Arrest Rose Blackwood before she kills someone!"

"Put her in a catapult and fire her into New Mexico Territory!"

"Ban her from the country!"

"Ban her from the planet!"

"Is anyone going to eat that leftover pie?"

Alright, that last one was me. I can't help it. I get hungry when I'm upset.

"Rose Blackwood needs to be stopped for good!"

"Who knows what she's planning on doing next? Any one of us could end up being her next victim!"

"She'll put all of your children in danger!"

"She'll steal the gold fillings from your great grandma's teeth!"

"But my great grandma doesn't have any teeth."

"That's not the point, Karen!"

"Rose Blackwood is the foulest criminal in the west!"

"Rose Blackwood is public enemy number one!"

"Rose Blackwood is to blame!"

"Excuse me? Did someone call my name?"

Every townsperson shut their mouth sharply at the same time, creating a very loud and very weird "*CLOP!*" sound, which echoed throughout the suddenly silent fairground. They slowly backed away, giving plenty of room to a woman whom they believed to be nothing short of deadly. Rose Blackwood stepped forward, looking uneasily at the residents of Pitchfork who trembled at the sight of her. Apparently, they were only comfortable saying terrible things about her when she wasn't there to hear them.

Now, here's something funny.

Well, it's not "ha ha" funny. I mean, you're not going to laugh out loud, unless of course you have a really strange sense of humor. Which you might. You might be the sort of person who sees a goat sneeze or watches an old man eat an onion, and then laughs like it's the funniest thing you've ever seen. I don't know. You could be very weird.

Anyway, the "funny" thing that I noticed was that Rose had changed her clothes again. She was once again dressed in the fancy outfit she'd been wearing back at the Baron Estate, with her face painted all sorts of unnaturally bright colors. Her hair was straightened, and she was carrying a little umbrella to shield her face from the sun.

She looked like, well, like a *lady*. It was very strange. I didn't like it. I liked Rose better when she dressed like Rose, in her black shirt, black pants, leather vest, cowboy hat,  and red boots with her initials printed on them. Aunt Dorcas had once asked Rose why she didn't wear dresses. "For the same reason you don't wear a cactus on your head. It's uncomfortable and silly," Rose had answered.

"Rose," M said slowly, "I want you to answer me truthfully. Did you enter a pie in the baking contest?"

Rose looked around and saw that the townspeople were all quietly awaiting her answer.

"Yes," she finally said, standing up straight and holding her chin up high. "I snuck in earlier and entered my pie without anyone noticing. So what if I did? It's not a crime to enter a pie in a contest."

"Is that true?" P whispered to M.

"Yes, dear, it's not a crime," M whispered back.

"But it is a crime to enter an *exploding* pie in the contest!" Madge Tweetie declared, her sopping wet hair plastered to the sides of her face. "Those flaming hot pears could have given me permanent scars on my beautiful face! I say that Rose Blackwood should be disqualified, arrested, tarred and feathered, and then forced to clean up this mess!"

She gestured towards the remains of pie and cake that had spattered the fairgrounds. It really was an awful and delicious mess.

"Shouldn't Rose be forced to clean the fairgrounds *before* she's tarred and feathered?" a townsperson suggested. "Otherwise she'll just make a big, sticky mess."

"Fine," Madge Tweetie said. "But we'll tar and feather her afterwards."

"Can we use something other than feathers?" Mr. Silva the blacksmith asked. "We've recently had a shortage of feathers because of all the pillows that the town has been making at the Pitchfork Pillow Factory. We wouldn't want to waste them. Maybe she can be tarred and *sanded* instead? We've got plenty of sand."

"Actually," another townsperson interrupted, "we're pretty short on tar too. We've started paving some new roads, and the tar that we have should really only be used for that. Maybe she can be *watered* and sanded instead?"

"We're in the middle of a drought!" yet another townsperson yelled. "We can't waste water on a criminal. She'll just have to be *sanded* and sanded."

Miss Danielle looked at Rose and frowned.

"She already has a bit of sand on her dress and in her hair," my teacher said. "It's been pretty windy today."

"Oh," said Madge Tweetie in a disappointed tone, before turning back to Rose. "Well . . . let that be a lesson to you."

"Wait a minute," Rose said as she walked over to my parents, ignoring the ugly looks that she was being given by the people of Pitchfork. "My pie actually exploded?"

"Not only did it explode," Aunt Dorcas said with a pout, "it destroyed all of the other pies that were entered in the contest too! Now no one can judge who the real winner should have been, even though we all know that it clearly should have been me."

My father went over to the remains of the tray that Rose Blackwood's explosive pie had been resting on, and he began to study it. He dipped his finger into the ash left behind, and then licked it.

"Hmmm," he murmured to himself. "Very interesting."

"What is it?" I asked. "Did you find a clue?"

"No. I just realized that I forgot to wash my hands this morning."

"Rose, dear," M said, "I'm afraid the people here believe that you might have sabotaged your pie. They think you rigged it to explode on purpose."

Rose's mouth dropped open in shock.

"What?" she gasped. "That's ridiculous! Who could think such a terrible thing?"

"Everyone!" Madge Tweetie said with a sneer. "If you hadn't blown up the competition, my pie would have been named the best pie in the fair. I would have been the first person in twenty years to have a winning tart and a winning pie in the same contest."

"I call shenanigans on that!" Aunt Dorcas bellowed. "Madge, your sloppy tarts might have fooled the judges, but there's no way that your pie would beat mine in a fair contest!"

Madge took her blue ribbon and shook it at my aunt.

"No need to be a sore loser, Dorcas," Madge taunted. "Everyone knows that your pies and tarts taste like sawdust and cow chips!"

"You shut your big bazoo, Madge!"

"No, *you* shut *your* big bazoo, Dorcas!"

As my aunt and her best friend continued to insult each other, I noticed that Rose was getting angrier and angrier by the moment. But strangely enough, the anger appeared to be directed at the only two adults in town who hadn't called for her to be locked away in jail forever: my mother and father.

"Mrs. Baron," Rose said to my mother in a voice that shook with emotion, "you can't possibly believe that I would ever try to hurt anyone."

"Well, dear," M said, looking very uncomfortable, "your pies and cakes have been rather . . . *unpredictable* lately. I still haven't been able to get the stink of your last cake out of the kitchen curtains. And you might have permanently stained the oven a strange shade of green with your last pie as well."

"What does that have to do with anything?" Rose cried, looking madder than an old wet hen. "It's one thing to burn a dessert or stink up some curtains, and it's another thing entirely to bake a pie that's meant to explode. I'm not a villain!"

"I'm not saying you are!" M argued. "I'm saying that you might have accidentally added some ingredients to your pie that caused it to explode! It *was* your pie that exploded, Rose, that's a fact. We all saw it."

"Hmmm," P murmured to himself again. "*Very* interesting."

"What is it this time?" I asked. "You forgot to wash your feet too?"

My father had gathered some more of the ash, as well as the charred remains of the exploding pie crust, and the blackened pie tin.

"There are traces of explosives in here," P announced. "This exploding pie wasn't an accident. Whoever did this, did it on purpose."

I gulped as I glanced over at Rose, who looked shocked by what my father had just said.

"Are you sure, P?" I asked quietly.

Instead of answering me with a yes or no, he reached into his pocket and produced a match. He lit it and put the match head to the pile, which immediately sizzled and spat sparks. He was right. There were definitely traces of explosive powder. This wasn't a recipe *gone bad*, it was an explosion *gone good*. Or something like that.

Sorry, I guess that sounded better in my head.

Rose's painted lower lip began to quiver. She stared at the pile of explosive powder in disbelief, and then she turned to my mother.

"Mrs. Baron," she said, "thank you for allowing me to work for you and your husband. It was a wonderful experience and a dream come true. It's the first time I've ever felt like I was a part of a family. I quit."

As my mother accepted Rose's resignation, one of the deputies came by and placed a set of handcuffs on her wrists.

"Rose Blackwood," the deputy said, "you are under arrest."

My parents and I were silent for the entire horseless carriage ride back home. My mother buried her face in her hands, while my father steered the carriage with a troubled look on his face. Aunt Dorcas muttered about her wasted pies and tarts, and how no one in town had any taste. I lay in the backseat and tried to keep my moaning to myself. My stomach was still in awful shape from all the pie and fair food I'd eaten, and the carriage ride wasn't helping. Every bump we hit felt like a fist to my swollen belly. It seemed wrong that something I loved so much could have hurt me so badly—and by that I meant both Rose Blackwood *and* pie.

B.W. had offered to ride Geoffrey back to the Baron Estate for us. He'd missed most of the excitement following the explosion, because he was using the outhouse at the time. He couldn't believe it when we'd told him that it looked as though Rose Blackwood had finally turned as evil as her brother.

"But she's nothing like Benedict Blackwood," B.W. had said, as he shook his head in disbelief. "I've read all about him in Sheriff Hoyt Graham's books. Rose is kind and sweet and generous, and Benedict is cruel and evil and greedy. There must be some sort of mistake."

But it didn't seem as though there had been a mistake, no matter how badly we all wished otherwise. Rose was the closest thing I'd ever had to a sister, and though she'd only been staying with us for a few months, we all considered her an honorary member of the Baron family. I was going to miss her terribly.

When we pulled up to the Baron Estate, P and M had to roll me out of the carriage like a barrel full of rainwater. I was so bloated with pie that two of my shirt buttons had popped off and hit Aunt Dorcas on the back of the head during the carriage ride.

"I think your supper tonight will be some light vegetable broth," M told me as she helped me up the front steps to the house. "And then some weak tea."

"Could we drop some chicken and dumplings into the vegetable broth?" I asked hopefully."And maybe serve the tea with a little cake or two?"

M stared at me for a moment, before slowly shaking her head as we went inside.

I guess that meant no.

The following week was filled with loneliness. When I went to school the next day, I found out that B.W. had come down with a terrible and contagious flu, which meant he would be staying out of school for a while, and I wouldn't be able to visit him. Shorty was still spending all her time with her father, who was having a difficult time coping with the fact that he would never be able to grow the thick and bushy mustache of his dreams. Aunt Dorcas was pouting because she had lost the contest, and because her best friend Madge Tweetie had spread a nasty rumor all over town that Dorcas had helped Rose bake her exploding pie.

And Rose, of course, was gone. She was locked up in

the Pitchfork jail. Her trial would be coming up soon, and I hoped that she would be proven innocent. I couldn't imagine her doing anything evil, I really couldn't. The thought of her stuck in a lonely jail cell made me terribly sad.

My parents refused to talk about Rose. They were quite upset that an assistant of theirs had been linked to a horrible crime, and they grew even more upset anytime that I mentioned her name. They were so upset about the whole exploding pie incident that they refused to talk about anything that had happened at the fair. In fact, my parents were barely speaking at all, except for a couple of words during mealtimes. Following the fair, M and P spent most of their time quietly tinkering with the inventions and devices in their work garage. I asked if they were working on a new and exciting invention that could lead us on another adventure, perhaps something that would send us up to the stars, or down into the center of the earth, or something that could allow us to travel back in time to prevent a terrible explosion from happening at a certain local fair.

"I'm afraid not," M told me with a sigh as she tinkered with a metal contraption that looked like a miniature cannon. "It looks like a lot of our old inventions have begun to fail, so we're just repairing them. You're welcome to stay and help us if you like. I could explain some of the inventions to you, so you can understand how to properly fix them. Take this invention, for instance. I explained to your friend B.W. that this particular invention is a rapid-fire gun, which actually makes new bullets while it's firing. It does that through—"

"That's alright," I said quickly, before the wacky music could start playing in my head. "I think I'll just go for a walk."

"Ask Geoffrey if he wants to go with you!" P called. "He worries that you and he haven't really bonded yet. Be nice to your new brother, W.B., he's a good horse."

"I talked to Geoffrey earlier today. He said that he was feeling a little tired and wanted to take a nap. But we promised to bond with each other later."

In truth, I had not spoken to the horse, mostly because you can't have a real conversation with a horse, unless you happen to have a mind as odd as my father's.

I just felt the need to clear that up.

I went for a walk on my own, past the border of the Baron Estate, and down the path which cut through the Pitchfork Desert and led into town. I'm not usually the sort of person who enjoys walking, because why waste time walking when there are sandwiches to be eaten? But I was lonely and bored and upset. And sitting by myself in the house only reminded me of my loneliness and boredom and upset feelings. I decided to see what nature had in store for me.

It was a lovely day, but I really wasn't in the mood for a lovely day. When I'm in a bad mood, I want to see dark clouds and thunderstorms, and flurries of snow and ice, or at the very least, the sort of powerful winds strong enough to lift a cow in the air and set it gently on your neighbor's roof. But, unfortunately, everything was just lovely in the Pitchfork Desert. It was bright and sunny. There was a nice, cool breeze in the air, and there were actually song-birds chirping in the sky instead of squawking vultures and crows.

As I walked down the desert path, I grumbled to myself about how annoying it was that everything was so sickeningly nice and lovely.

And because I was so busy grumbling, I didn't notice that someone had snuck up behind me. They grabbed me by the neck and threw a heavy sack over my head so I couldn't see. I was then hit over the head so hard that I could actually feel my back teeth vibrate from the impact, and soon pink and purple squirrels were performing cart-wheels in my slowly swimming mind. As I fell to the ground and began to slip into unconsciousness, I tried to

call for help. But the only sound my mouth made was
MERRrrrgggg . . .

Bouncing Halfway Across the Country on My Backside

"MERRrrrgggg . . ." I merggged as my eyes began to flutter.

"Did you hear that?" a strange voice asked. "The little feller merggged again."

"He sure does a lot of merggging, don't he?" another strange voice answered.

Once my eyes were open and adjusted to the light, I found myself feeling quite confused, which was actually pretty normal for me. I'm often confused. In fact, sometimes I get a bit concerned if I'm not confused. It just doesn't feel right.

But this time I was more confused than usual.

I was lying on a splintered wood floor. I could see several bales of hay stacked across from me. I smelled animals, but strangely enough, I couldn't see any animals. I did see two men though, who were dressed in shabby coats, shoes with holes in the toe, wrinkled ties that were cut in half, stained shirts without collars, vests missing half the buttons, and high hats with holes punched into the top. They were looking at me with amused expressions on their dirty and unshaven faces.

At first I thought that I must have stumbled into a barn, but then I noticed that the barn appeared to be moving.

"Is this a movable room?" I asked the men, and then winced when my hand accidentally brushed against the back of my head.

There was a big lump there from when I'd been hit. I must have been hit really, really hard. I've had many heavy things land on my head before (a bookshelf, an anvil, a cannon ball, a baby grand piano, a wheelbarrow filled with turnips, a goat, a shed), but this felt like the biggest beating that my hard head had ever taken.

"I suppose you could call it that," one of the men said with a toothless grin. "Ain't you never been on a dangler before, buckaroo?"

"My name is W.B.," I told him as I struggled to stand, then gave up and remained seated. "What's a 'dangler'? It sounds gross, like something that's hanging out of your nose that you don't know about."

"A dangler is an express train, kid."

"A train?" I repeated. "Oh. No, I've never been on a train before."

"Well, you're on one now!" the other one cackled, slapping his knee with his palm. "The Old 44 Express! The fastest dangler in the U.S. of A! Hah hee!"

"Hah hee!" the other man echoed.

"Hah hee!" I echoed too, though I didn't know why. "Wait, why am I on a train?"

"Good question, chickabiddy," one of the cackling men said as he sat down beside me and pulled out a pocket knife and a can of Newer Oldtown Old Fashioned Beans. "When we hopped aboard to beat the road, we found you lying here, unconscious. I'm not usually a betting man,

but I'd be willing to bet all the tulips in Tallahassee that someone knocked you on the noggin and then dumped you in here. I bet the feller who did that to you most likely wanted to get you out of the way. Looks like you made yourself an enemy, jackeroo."

Knocked me on the noggin and dumped me in here? Get me out of the way? Made an enemy? Tulips in Tallahassee? Jackeroo?

"What do you mean by *get me out of the way*?" I asked.

"He means that the person who bonked you on the cabbage and tossed you into this train car must have wanted you on the other side of the country as quickly as possible, probably so you couldn't cause them any trouble," the other man explained, as he pulled out a box of crackers. "We see it happen all the time. You must have seen something you shouldn't have seen, or heard something that you shouldn't have heard, or smelled something you shouldn't have smelled, or tasted something you shouldn't have tasted, and now someone wants to get you out of the picture, understand?"

"No," I said, my throbbing brain still spinning in my skull. "I don't understand any of that. Smelled something I shouldn't have smelled? What?"

"You know too much, kid, much too much," one of the

men said while he opened the can of baked beans with his knife. "And trust me, I know what I'm talking about. My name is Lefty."

Lefty bowed, and pointed to the man holding the box of crackers.

"And he's Lefty Also. You look like you're hungry, little lubber, though you strike me as the sort of feller who's always hungry, ain't you? I mean, your eyes ain't left this can of baked beans since I pulled it from my pocket. Would you like some beans on crackers? You might not believe me, but I know from personal experience that beans on crackers is the preferred breakfast of the kings over in Europe."

I didn't believe him. First of all, he pronounced "Europe" like "your-oppy," which I was pretty sure wasn't correct. Secondly, I'd met several kings in Europe during my last adventure with my parents, and I didn't see a single one of them eating baked beans on crackers. But I still thanked Lefty and Lefty Also for their generosity. The way that the orange-colored sun slowly began to pour through the lone window of the chugging train car led me to believe that I must have been unconscious for quite some time. It was the early hours of the morning, and I was very hungry.

I ate all the crackers and beans that Lefty and Lefty Also gave to me, as well as some that they didn't—I sneaked them while they weren't looking. While I ate the beans and crackers, they told me all about their fascinating lives.

"Well, let me tell you a thing or two about a thing or three," Lefty Also began, leaning back and crossing his hands behind his head. "We weren't  always drifters, me and Lefty. In fact, we used to be successful and respected members of society, the biggest toads in the puddle, believe it or not."

"Not," I said.

"Don't interrupt me, tenderfoot. You see, back in the old days, Lefty and I used to attend all sorts of fancy parties and fancy dinners, and we'd stay in fancy hotels, while dressed up in our fancy clothes without any holes or mysterious stains on them. By the way, what do you think this mysterious stain on my shoulder is? Mustard? I hope it's mustard. I've been licking it all morning. Anyway, Lefty and I used to be *world famous inventors*."

"Oh really?" I asked, sneaking another cracker. "You

don't say."

"I *do* say. And stop sneaking crackers."

"Sorry."

"We invented wonderful and fantastic things that the world had never seen before," Lefty Also continued, as he put the rest of the crackers in his pocket. "Our most famous invention was an indoor outhouse that we built over thirty-five years ago."

"How did you build that?" I asked, thinking about our own indoor bathroom at the Baron Estate, which my parents had designed and built long before I was born. "Did you attach lots of pipes filled with water that lead outdoors into an underground metal tank?"

"Nope, we just put a regular outhouse inside a house," Lefty answered. "No pipes. No water. No tanks. No nothing. We just cut a big hole in the floor and placed the outhouse on top of it. As it turns out, it wasn't a very good invention. In fact, it was pretty terrible. The people who had our indoor outhouses built in their homes said they were disgusting. And they were right, by gum. After a few days, their houses all stunk pretty badly."

"Very badly," Lefty Also agreed. "The indoor outhouses also attracted a lot of flies. In fact, they attracted so many flies that we were forced to invent a *bug zapper* to get rid of them all."

"What's a 'bug zapper'?" I asked.

"It's an invention that we came up with, which gets rid of pesky bugs. What you do is take a stick, dip it into kerosene, and then you light the end of the stick on fire. Then, when you see a bug in your house, you hit it with the flaming stick and yell 'ZAP!'"

"ZAP!" Lefty echoed, cackling wildly.

"Isn't that dangerous?" I asked.

"It was incredibly dangerous!" Lefty Also exclaimed. "In fact, everyone who used our bug zapper ended up burning down their home."

"It *did* get rid of the bugs though," Lefty assured me.

"That's right," Lefty Also nodded. "But folks still got angry with us and demanded that we give them money to buy new homes. People care way too much about money, in my humble opinion. Well, by that point, Lefty and I were broke. We didn't have a tailfeather left between us. So we decided to quit inventing things. Instead, we would live life on the road, as two merry drifters, traveling across the country with no home, job, family, or crippling lawsuits to weigh us down. We're making hay while the sun shines. Some might call us hobos or bums, but I prefer to use the word drifter or traveler. It just sounds better."

"Yep," Lefty confirmed. "We're just two merry travelers who are on a mission to see every inch of this great land, traveling by the skin of our teeth. This is a mighty big country, and a high-speed train is the best way to see as much of it as you can, as quickly as you can. You'd be amazed how fast this dangler travels."

Lefty opened the sliding door of the train car and tossed the empty bean can outside. I could see that we were riding across a long, grassy area that I didn't recognize. It didn't look like any part of Arizona Territory.

"Where are we?" I asked.

"That's a darn good question, little shaver," Lefty said as he peered across the fields, which appeared to run all the way to the horizon. "If I had to guess, and I tell you I ain't no fancy guessing feller, I'd have to say that we're somewhere in the northern part of the great state of Texas."

"*Texas?!*" I gasped.

My mind immediately tried to form a map of the country, to figure out how far from home I was. Unfortunately, it wasn't a particularly good map. It was a big splotchy picture, shaped sort of like a pie, with Pitchfork in the dead center. The inaccuracy of my mental map wasn't entirely my fault. If we spent more time studying maps and less time on silly oral reports in school, then I'm sure I'd be better at geography. The shape of my mental map would be more accurate and a lot less pie-shaped.

I didn't know quite where Texas was, but I knew that it was far from home, and that I was in a lot of trouble.

"That's right, kid," Lefty Also told me as he patted me on the back. "Good old Texas. *The Two Star State*, as they call it. I can tell from the way that your eyeballs have grown that you ain't been to Texas before. This must be really exciting for you!"

"Hah hee!" Lefty cackled.

"Hah hee!" Lefty Also echoed.

"Hah hee," I echoed sadly.

Exciting was not the word I would have used.

"I don't suppose you know when this train stops next?" I asked the two merry drifters.

"Good question, kid," Lefty Also said.

"Thanks. I'm terrible with answers, but I'm usually pretty good with questions."

"This train won't stop until it reaches Chicago," Lefty explained. "We still have a long ways to go until then, ya little scamp. We still need to pass through Oklahoma Territory, Kansas, and Missouri."

Chicago? I knew where Chicago was. I had traveled there once before with my family, and I knew firsthand that it was *very* far from home. It took several hours to get there by flying house, which meant it would take even longer to get there by train.

"But I need to get off this train now!" I cried. "I can't go to Chicago! I need to get home to Pitchfork! I'm missing several very important meals!"

"Sorry, scrappy, you won't be going anywhere anytime soon, except where the Old 44 Express takes you. Why don't you kick back and relax? Put your feet up for a spell."

How was I expected to kick back and relax when I was stuck on a train that was quickly traveling all the way across the country, and I had absolutely no idea how I'd ever get home? How could I put my feet up for a spell when my situation was literally getting worse by the second?

"Isn't there anyone I can talk to? Someone who can stop the train so I can get off? Maybe I can find someone in one of the other cars who can help me, like the train conductor."

Lefty and Lefty Also each raised an eyebrow at me as their toothless smiles quickly melted into gummy frowns. Suddenly, they didn't look so friendly.

"Kid, we ain't exactly on this train legally, if you know what I mean," Lefty said quietly. "And neither are you. No one in this train car has a ticket. That means you should avoid the train conductor, understand? If you go off in search of him, and he kicks me and Lefty Also off this train, we're not going to be very happy with you, understand?"

I nodded quickly. I understood perfectly well.

I was trapped.

I had no money, which meant that when the train finally stopped in Chicago, I wouldn't be able to pay to send a message to my family. The only people I knew who lived in Chicago, Shorty and her folks, were currently staying in Pitchfork, so there was no one in the city who could help me. And I wasn't clever enough to think of anything else to do. I had no way home. I would have to become a merry traveler like Lefty and Lefty Also, hoping that one day I'd sneak onto a westbound train that happened to pass through Pitchfork. I wondered if by the time I finally got home, I'd have holes in my shoes, a long grey beard, and a wacky laugh, just like the Leftys. Knowing my luck, I probably would. Mine would probably be extra wacky.

"Good lad," Lefty said, as he patted me on the head. "I knew you were smarter than you looked, shanny. Now, I think it's time that Lefty Also and I showed you how we like to pass the hours while we're riding the Old 44

Express across the country."

Lefty looked over at Lefty Also and winked. Lefty Also winked back. They both hopped up and dusted off their incredibly dusty jackets, which made me cough for almost a minute straight. And then they started to sing.

"A-one, and a-two, and a-one-two-three . . . *the Camptown ladies sing this song, doo-dah! Doo-dah! The Camptown racetrack's five miles long! Oh de doo-dah-dey! Goin' to run all night! Goin' to run all day! I bet my money on a bob-tailed nag! Somebody bet on the grey!*"

The merry travelers started dancing up a storm while singing "Camptown Races," a song that used to be one of my favorites.

Used to be.

I'd heard that song so many times that I never wanted to hear it again. I'd grown quite sick of it. And even before I'd grown sick of it, I wouldn't have wanted to hear it sung the way that Lefty and Lefty Also were singing it. It turned out that the merry travelers were even worse singers than they were inventors, which gives you an idea of the agony I was in as I sat there and listened to them screech and howl off-key, searching for a tune which they couldn't find with both hands and a map, no matter how hard they tried. They also didn't know all the words to the song, so they just repeated the first two verses over and over and over again, slapping their knees, kicking their feet, then slapping their feet and kicking their knees. The Old 44 Express chugged along as we sped further away from my home and closer to a nightmare that was already looking unbearable.

When the merry travelers started the song over again for the forty-fifth time, I finally did something crazy. I had to. Their singing was turning my brain to mush. The sliding door to the train car was still wide open. I looked out at the rocky field that we were speeding through at a phenomenal pace. And then I looked over to the tone-deaf merry travelers, who didn't seem as though they were going to stop singing "Camptown Races" until we reached Chicago.

I screamed as loudly as I could, and I jumped.

I hit the ground and bounced, flipping end over end as my exhausted body met the grass and dirt and rocks, bouncing and tumbling and spinning and rolling until I was so dizzy that the dancing pink and purple squirrels I saw out of the corner of my eyes looked as though they were getting seasick. As I tumbled, I could still hear those horrible singing voices—"Camptown Races" echoing in the back of my brain like an off-key bell. When I finally stopped my somersaults and backflips, I looked up and saw the Old 44 Express riding off into the distance, chugging along without me, on its way to Chicago.

"Farewell, Lefty and Lefty Also," I muttered. "The memory of your kindness will live on in my heart. And the memory of your singing voices will live on in my nightmares."

Well, I had done it. I had escaped the train and survived the fall. I stood up on legs that felt as though they were made of melting butter and looked around. I was in a wide-open prairie, and when I say wide, I mean w i d e. There was nothing for miles except for more prairies, endless stretches of tall grass and dirt and rocks and bushes. It was late morning, the sun having already completed its trip over the horizon. As I looked around at the empty landscape, a cold breeze blew through my hair. Birds cawed, lizards scuttled, insects buzzed, and I was alone.

When I'm in a terrible and hopeless situation (which happens far too often, in my opinion), I sometimes find that the best thing to do is to pretend to be someone else, someone who is much smarter than me. Why do I do that, you ask? Well, because being far from home with no money or horse might seem like a hopeless situation for silly little W.B., but it wouldn't be a problem for my brilliant father. What if P was in my situation? What would he do? How would he save himself? If I could think like my brilliant and creative father, then I could come up with a way to get back home.

I mussed up my hair into pointy spikes and pretended that I was him.

I looked down and spotted a little prairie dog and was immediately overwhelmed by the urge to make it a hat.

H m m m m .

Maybe I shouldn't pretend to be P, I thought. *He might be brilliant, but he's also terribly silly and easily distracted, and, without someone like my mother there to guide him, he wasn't going to be much help.*

Next, I pretended to be my mother, though I had to stop pretending to be her after only a few minutes because I kept feeling so disappointed in W.B. for his lack of interest in science, as well as his ridiculous obsession with pie.

Then I pretended to be Aunt Dorcas, and after I had finished yelping and crying and screaming like a hyena with diaper rash, I realized that I wasn't making much progress towards fixing my situation. It's really not very productive being Aunt Dorcas. I promised myself to tell her that if I ever saw her again.

I also pretended to be Shorty, B.W., Miss Danielle, and Magnus (our old horse). None of those were helpful either, though pretending to be Magnus gave me the idea to eat some of the tall grass surrounding me, so I wasn't quite as hungry as I was before. Good old Magnus. I missed that horse.

As I scanned my brain for another person to pretend to be, I couldn't help but think of the person who had, until recently, been a very close friend of mine, someone whom I admired greatly: Rose Blackwood.

Rose. I still couldn't believe that she was in jail. The

Rose Blackwood that I knew wouldn't harm a fly. I thought about the time when she had saved my life. It was several months earlier, and we were traveling across the country in our flying house. I was about to be stomped by a pack of wild pigs, and Rose had used her only bullet to save me. She had fired her gun straight into the air instead of shooting at the wild pigs because she didn't like the idea of hurting them either. She didn't have to do that. But she did. Because Rose Blackwood wasn't a killer, nor was she evil, or capable of harming people who didn't deserve it.

The more I thought about her, the more I wished that my family and I had taken the time to listen to Rose's side of the story. And I really wished that we had defended her from the accusations hurled at her by the people of Pitchfork. Rose had told us that she considered the Barons to be her family, and I knew for certain that I thought of her as an older sister, and family was supposed to stick together. We were supposed to give each other the benefit of the doubt. And I was ashamed of the fact that we hadn't.

As I stood beside the train tracks, thinking about Rose and what my family should have done after the explosion at the Pitchfork Fair, my mind was so distracted that I didn't notice the sound of the westbound train approaching.

The conductor and engineer must have been blowing the horn repeatedly as the train chugged towards me, but I didn't hear it. Sometimes, when I'm deep in thought, I don't notice anything that's happening around me, and sometimes that gets me into trouble. Like the time when I was deep in thought while roasting a hot dog on a stick and ended up with my arm catching on fire. Or like the time when I was cooking pancakes while deep in thought and ended up with my arm catching on fire. Or like the time when I was pickling eggs while deep in thought and both of my arms ended up catching on fire.

But this time, being deep in thought managed to save my life. As the train roared by, the railing of the caboose snagged my suspenders, lifting me up into the air, and pulling me along for the ride. Before I knew what was happening, I was on my way home, bouncing halfway across the country on my backside.

I'D BET MY BIG TOE ON IT

I don't know how much time passed before the west-bound train finally arrived in Arizona Territory. I was black and blue from bouncing along the tracks. The lower half of my body had gone numb. My hair was a mess of dirt and leaves and twigs. My face was covered with a thick layer of soot. Every time I coughed, a cloud of smoke puffed out of my mouth like I was a miniature steam engine.

I had screamed for most of the train ride home and finally lost my voice somewhere around New Mexico Territory. It was for the best. I was getting pretty sick of the sound of my screams by that point and needed a little peace and quiet. When the train finally pulled into the Pitchfork train station, and I recognized where I was, I was so overjoyed and relieved that, after I unhooked my suspenders from the railing of the caboose, I did my family's happy dance.

My family's happy dance is a very silly dance that we do when we're happy. It feels good to do it, though I've been told it makes us look like freshly caught fish that are desperately trying to get back into the water. As I happy-danced, a few people who were walking by dropped some coins into my cap, which had fallen off my head. I realized that they probably thought I was a street performer, who was putting on a show for them. I continued to dance, and a few more people dropped some coins into my cap and smiled at me.

Hmmm . . .

I figured if I kept dancing, and people kept giving me coins, I might be able to make enough money to pay a horse and carriage driver, so I wouldn't have to walk all the way back to the Baron Estate. Maybe I'd be able to afford a decent meal in town too—it felt like *ages* since I'd had a decent meal. So I kept dancing, putting my heart and soul into it, doing all sorts of fancy dances that I'd seen performed around the world, dances like "the purple German," "the swollen kneecap," "the one-man polka," "the itchy fish trot," and the infamous "stinky onion," dancing with more energy than I ever had before, spinning and whooping as I moved to the strange rhythms in my mind.

"That poor boy," I heard one lady whisper to another, as they each placed a penny in my cap. "Hopefully, with that money, he'll be able to see a doctor who can fix whatever it is that's wrong with him."

"I know," the other lady responded. "Perhaps he'll be able to afford a decent haircut as well."

I took the money from the hat and stuffed it into my pockets, and then stuffed my head into my cap. I no longer felt like dancing.

"What's wrong with my haircut?" I muttered to myself, as I pulled a bit of cacti from my cowlick.

I set about crossing the desert, following the long and lonesome road through the sandy dunes which led back to the Baron Estate. I was exhausted, and shivering, and, more than that, I was *starving*. I couldn't remember the last time I'd eaten. Well, actually, I could. It was the beans and crackers that Lefty and Lefty Also had given me on the train, followed by the tall grass I'd eaten when I was pretending to be our old horse Magnus. But that was barely a snack, and I was a growing boy who needed to eat six or fifteen square meals a day to survive. As I trekked through the desert, I began to see food everywhere. Cacti began to look like hot dogs. Rocks began to look like fried chicken. Sand dunes began to look like mashed potatoes. My hand began to look like a ham sandwich. My feet like a pair of dill pickles. My knees like a pair of cabbages, which I don't particularly like, though they might be tasty if eaten with my ham sandwich hands. If I hadn't spotted the white picket fence surrounding the Baron Estate, I might have done something really weird, which I would have regretted.

I was so excited to be home that I forgot all about my appetite for a moment (well, sort of—I planned on running inside and greeting everyone while swiftly making my way to the kitchen, where I'd make a sandwich so large that it would take three or four plates to carry), and I started to jog towards the house.

I made it about halfway there before I spotted something that made my heart stop.

Geoffrey the horse galloped around the corner of the Baron Estate. And on his back, was me.

Yes. *Me.* That wasn't a typo.

I stared at myself riding on the horse with ease and wondered how I'd managed to overcome my clumsiness.

Normally, I couldn't ride a horse longer than a few minutes before I'd somehow fall off or get tangled in the saddle or end up with my head lodged in the horse's mouth. But then I realized that the person sitting on the horse couldn't possibly be me, because *I* was me, or at least I was pretty certain that I was me. If I wasn't me, then I'd definitely have some explaining to do to myself.

The me sitting on the horse then spotted the me that was me. I made eye contact with myself, and for a moment, neither of me moved.

The W.B. sitting on the horse looked exactly like me, right down to my funny cowlick. He was even dressed in one of my collarless shirts, with suspenders that were slightly tangled. I looked down and saw that the suspenders I was wearing were slightly tangled as well. At least I had an excuse. I doubted that the W.B. on the horse was just dragged halfway across the country.

Finally, because I didn't know what else to do, I waved to myself.

"Hi," I said in a choked voice. "Looking good."

My voice was choked because I was exhausted, and because I was thirsty, and because I had inhaled a lot of dust, dirt, smoke, garbage, and bugs while I was being pulled by the train. I also might have been coming down with a cold. You know how you're supposed to wear a jacket when you go out at night to avoid getting sick? Well, you should also definitely wear one while being dragged across the country at fifty miles per hour.

"Hi," said the me sitting on the horse, who, after giving me a mysterious little wink, turned towards the house and screamed. "Hey! M! P! He's back again! The person who's been watching me! Hurry!"

I stared at myself in confusion, wondering what me meant by that, when suddenly my parents came bursting through the front door. My mother had a broomstick in her hand, and my father had a large pot and a wooden spoon. They rushed towards me with anger in their eyes.

"Hi," I croaked. "Any chance I could get a sandwich or six?"

"Get out of here!" M shouted as she swung her broomstick. "You get out of here now, or I'll get the sheriff!"

"Huh?"

"Get away from here!" P cried, banging the pot with the spoon as he shouted. "You're not welcome!"

"But, I'm . . . I'm W.B.," I wheezed, not knowing what else to say.

I coughed again. My voice sounded as raspy and croaky as a frog with bronchitis. My face was caked with dirt and dust. No wonder they didn't recognize me. I barely recognized me.

My mother swung her broomstick at me. I ducked, and quickly backed away.

"I *told you* that someone was watching me!" the W.B. on the horse told my parents. "I was out here, bonding with Geoffrey, when suddenly he appeared at the fence! He told me that if I didn't give him all of our money, food, and dangerous inventions, that he'd do something terrible to us!"

"What?" I choked, ducking again as my mother continued to swing the broomstick at me. "I didn't say any of that! I wouldn't mind a bit of food though."

Geoffrey whinnied angrily at me, bucking his legs and snorting. In all the time that I'd known that horse, I'd never seen him react that way. He looked angry, and worse than that, he was giving me the appearance of being a dangerous stranger who did not belong at the Baron Estate. P once told me that animals are excellent at detecting when a person is evil, and I suppose that's usually true. But the horse had it all backwards this time. Maybe I should have bonded with him before. Why did I have to lie to my father about talking to that horse?

"You've upset Geoffrey!" my father bellowed. "Now it's

personal! Upset my son? Fine. Upset my wife? Well, that's still not nice, but I can live with that too. But upset my horse? Then we have a problem! Go away and never come back, or I'll shrink you to the size of a bug and then squash you!"

Perhaps because of how angry he looked, or perhaps because I knew he could actually do what he'd just threatened to do, I turned and ran away.

As I was running through the Pitchfork Desert, it suddenly occurred to me what had happened.

For me to explain it to you, I'll have to jump back in time, back to the end of my last adventure with my family . . .

Several Weeks Earlier, While Sitting in the Baron Estate Kitchen

"I have never seen anyone eat a banana cream pie that fast," Rose said, shaking her head in wonder. "Did you even take time to chew it, or did you just force it down your throat like a pelican?"

I held in a burp as I shrugged.

"I was hungry."

"You're *always* hungry."

"What's your point?" I asked, holding in another burp.

Sometimes Rose asked the silliest questions.

We were sitting across from each other at the kitchen table, and just as I was about to ask her what time she thought we would be having dinner, I heard yelling from outside.

"W.B.! Rose! Come out here!" my mother called, "We have something exciting to show you!"

Rose looked at me and winked. I burped. She rolled her eyes as she slipped on her red cowboy boots and dragged me outside.

We took three steps out the back door before we froze in utter shock.

"What?" Rose said.

"Huh?" I said.

"Hello, Rose and W.B.," my mother said.

"W.B. and Rose, hello," my mother said.

My mother was standing in front of the work garage. And standing beside her was my mother. There were two Ms. They were identical, right down to the work clothes and little round glasses. I rubbed my eyes with my knuckles to make sure I wasn't seeing double. Sometimes my eyes just needed a good rubbing in order to see properly. I looked again. Nope. I still had two mothers.

"How are you doing this?" Rose whispered.

My mother looked at herself and both of her laughed.

"Excellent question, Rose," one of my mothers said, before pulling out a little device that looked like a mechanical loaf of bread with two buttons on it. "Sharon and I have invented something new and fantastic. It is perhaps the most fantastic thing we've ever invented in our whole inventing careers. It will change the world forever."

Up to that point, my parents had invented a flying house, an invention that makes things bigger, an invention that makes things smaller, a horseless carriage, a coal powered underwater ship, a rocket that could fly to the stars, a giant magnet (which we aren't allowed to talk about), and yet this was the first inventions of theirs that had left me speechless.

"Huh?" I said, looking from

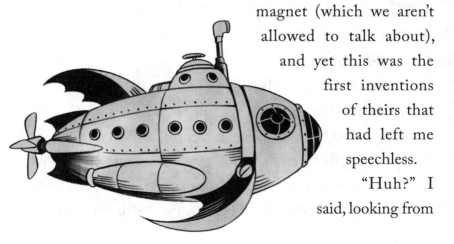

my mother, back over to my mother, and then back to my other mother again. I was starting to feel dizzy, as though I might fall over at any moment, which I then did. Rose had to help me to my feet.

"We have invented the Doppelgänger Device!" one of my mothers said proudly.

"I wanted to name it the S.A.Y.S. Device, or the *Same-As-You, Stephen* Device, but your mother wouldn't let me," said my other mother, who was clearly my father.

"Mr. Baron?" Rose gasped. "Is that really you?"

"I'm pretty certain that it is," said my father, who looked and sounded exactly like my mother. "Allow me to explain how this new device works. It's really quite simple! All you need to do is point the Doppelgänger Device at a person and press *this* button. Then, you point the Doppelgänger Device at yourself and press *this* button, and it will transform you into the other person."

"Wow . . ." Rose breathed.

"Wow indeed," said my mother (who was actually my mother), who then pointed to a small, circular glass panel on the underside of the invention. "The Doppelgänger Device also keeps track of every time that it's copied a person. All you have to do is look into this little glass panel, and it will show you who has been copied, and how many times they've been copied. We felt that we needed something to record that information, so we *can* tell if it's been used by someone other than us. Otherwise, a clever criminal could cause a lot of trouble with this invention."

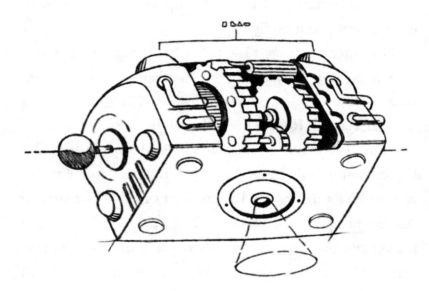

I finally found my voice again. It was right where I had left it, in the back of my throat.

"How long does it last?" I asked. "This isn't going to be permanent, is it? Not that I'm complaining, but it would make M's birthday a bit confusing."

"It isn't permanent," my father said, using one hand to brush back his long hair. "It only lasts for a few hours, six or seven at the most. I'm tinkering with a way to reverse the effects of the Doppelgänger Device immediately, but so far, there have been some problems."

"What sort of problems?" Rose asked.

My father bit his lip nervously.

"Let's just say that I'm glad I tested it on a tree before I tested it on myself."

It was the Doppelgänger Device! It had to be! Someone was staying at the Baron Estate and posing as me! They must have knocked me over the head and thrown me onto the train to get me out of the picture, so they could then pose as me! Lefty and Lefty Also were right! The crazy hobos were brighter than they seemed, even though they were tone-deaf, and had a baffling lack of understanding when it came to personal hygiene and modern plumbing.

But who would want me out of the picture? And why? And how did they know about the Doppelgänger Device? And what was their final plan?

I wondered all those things as I crossed the desert and entered Downtown Pitchfork. I thought of the strange feeling I'd been getting lately, the feeling that someone was watching me. They must have been pointing the Doppelgänger Device at me so the device could copy my body. They were also probably studying my behavior, so they'd be able to do a good imitation of me once they got me out of the way and started to pose as W.B.

Though to be honest, it isn't particularly difficult to do a good W.B. impression. Trip a lot. Bonk your head. Eat some pie. Congratulations, you're me.

I didn't know what to do next, so I went to the hotel where Shorty and her parents were staying. Maybe my friend could give me some advice. She had already saved me once before, when Benedict Blackwood was about to use my head for target practice, and I knew that I could count on her.

But when I got to the hotel, the owner informed me that Shorty and her folks had gone to another hospital in a neighboring town, and that she didn't know when they would be returning. I left her a note to give to Shorty, and then, trying my luck, asked the hotel owner if she would mind if I waited for her to return, maybe spending the night and having a warm bath and a few hot meals on their bill. The owner, very politely, lifted me by my suspenders, and booted me out of the room.

I had a few coins in my pocket from dancing, but it was barely enough for me to afford a good meal. I thought about finding a crowded street corner and dancing again, to see if I could make enough money to afford a hotel room for the night. But when I tried, I found that the people on the busy streets of Pitchfork were done being generous to the funny looking boy with the bad haircut. They mostly just stared at me. One old lady threw mushy tomatoes at my head.

Then I was hit by an idea, as well as another tomato.

"I've stopped dancing," I told the old lady.

"I don't care!" she retorted, tossing her last tomato at me before waddling away.

There was one other person in town who I could still go and see. She probably wouldn't be able to help me, but I find that when I'm in trouble sometimes it helps to have a friend to talk to.

Even if that friend was currently in jail.

I walked into the Pitchfork jailhouse. It was the second time that I'd been there. The first time was when Shorty and I had rescued my parents and Rose Blackwood, who had been locked in the jailhouse by Benedict Blackwood and his evil gang. I can't say that I missed the place. It had a bit of charm, I guess, if you consider holes in the roof, mysterious puddles on the floor, and a smell that reminded you of unwashed dogs to be charming.

There was a deputy asleep in the corner with his feet up on his desk, his hat pulled down over his eyes. His snores echoed throughout the little jailhouse, which, at the moment, only had one prisoner: Rose Blackwood.

She was sitting on the bench of her jail cell, and the first thing I noticed was that she was blushing. Her cheeks and nose shone as brightly as her freshly polished boots, and she was giggling. Then I noticed the person standing outside of her cell: Deputy Buddy Graham.

He was blushing too.

I watched them for another few moments as they continued to laugh softly and blush like a giggly pair of overripe strawberries, before Rose caught a glimpse of me out of the corner of her eye.

"W.B.?" she asked with a frown. "Is that you? You look awful."

"You sure do," Deputy Graham said, as he brushed his red hair back from his forehead. "Kid, you look like someone just rolled you in all the way from Mississippi."

"Actually, it was Texas, but that doesn't matter. Rose, do you remember the Doppelgänger Device?"

Rose rolled her eyes.

"Are you seriously asking if I remember the invention that transformed your father into your mother for six hours? Of course I remember it. Why?"

I explained to her what I'd seen, how I was knocked over the head and thrown onto a cross country train, how I threw myself out of the train to escape the awful singing of the merry travelers, and how I had returned to the Baron Estate to find another W.B. posing as me.

My explanation probably sounded like the ravings of a madman. In fact, if it had been anyone other than Rose Blackwood listening to my explanation, they likely would have thought that I'd simply taken one too many lumps to the head.

Which I probably had. But that's another story.

"Who do you think it was?" she asked, when I'd finished explaining.

"I don't know. I was hoping you could help me figure that out."

Rose started to speak, but then she looked over to Deputy Buddy. The sheriff's son seemed terribly confused.

"This must all sound really crazy to you," she said to

him.

"I honestly didn't understand half of what the kid said," Buddy Graham admitted. "He must be really smart, just like his parents. My dad always told me that the Barons were geniuses."

"W.B. isn't smart like his parents. In fact, he's a little bit d—" Rose began, but then she stopped and cleared her throat when she remembered that I was standing right there. "I mean, he's a *different kind* of smart. Some people are *book smart*, which means they're very educated, like Mr. and Mrs. Baron. And some people are *street smart*, which means they have good instincts, like you and your father. And some people are *people smart*, which mean they're a good judge of character, like me. And then there's W.B."

"What kind of *smart* am I?" I asked.

"Umm . . ." Rose said, searching her mind for an answer. "You're . . . uh . . . I suppose you could be described as . . . umm . . . say, that's a very nice shirt you're wearing, W.B."

Deputy Buddy quickly nodded his head.

"She's right. Underneath all the dirt and soot and cow plop, you can tell it's a really fine quality shirt."

So apparently, I'm *shirt smart*? Great. I'm sure that'll come in handy one day.

"Thanks, guys. I'm going to need your help. M and P have already chased me away from the house. They think I'm some sort of sneak who's been creeping around the Baron Estate. I'll need you to convince them that I'm the real me, and that the other kid is a fake me."

"But if there are two of you, then how do we know for certain that *you're* the real W.B.?" Deputy Buddy asked.

I was about to answer him, but suddenly I lost my balance and fell backwards, knocking my head against the brick jailhouse wall.

"OW!"

I clutched my head and tried to stand up straight, but I was feeling a bit woozy from the bump on my head, so I stumbled forward, tripped over a bench, and somehow ended up getting my head stuck between the bars of one of the jail cells.

"Yup," said Rose as she slowly nodded her head. "That's the real W.B. I'd bet my big toe on it."

HE'S STARING AT HIS HAND AS THOUGH IT'S A HAM SANDWICH

It turns out that even though Rose and Deputy Buddy appeared to be getting along quite well, Sheriff Graham and the other people of Pitchfork still believed that she was responsible for the explosion at the fair. That meant she had to stay locked up in the jailhouse.

"I know that you would never do anything like that, Rose," Deputy Buddy told her. "But it won't be so easy to convince everyone else. My dad is still in the hospital because of the exploding pie."

"Do they need to plug up the hole in his head where the pen used to be?" I asked.

"Yup, though they're having a lot of trouble finding a pen that'll fit the hole as well as the other one did."

"Why don't they just sew up the hole and forget about the pen?" Rose asked.

Buddy and I both looked at her as though she was insane. Forget about the pen?

Psssh. There were some things that women just didn't understand . . .

"Anyway," Deputy Buddy said to Rose, "unless we can prove your innocence, I can't let you out of here."

He looked awfully sorry. Strangely enough, Rose looked a bit sorry as well.

"I understand," she said. "You're just doing your job, Buddy."

For a moment, we all stood there, feeling sorry for Rose and her awful predicament, when suddenly my brain sneezed.

"Idea!"

Rose and Deputy Buddy looked at me as though I'd just . . . well, as though I'd just jumped in the air and shouted "Idea!" Which I had. I don't get great ideas often, so it's sort of a shock to my body when I do. It felt like my brain had been tickled until it sneezed.

I guess my father was right. Having your brain tickled

wasn't necessarily a bad thing. Unless of course it starts a sneezing fit.

"I have an idea," I told them. "Rose, you're a terrible baker, maybe the worst baker in the history of the world. Your cakes and pies are so gross that we couldn't even get the wild desert dogs to eat them. They're so foul that the flies avoided them, and flies eat cow plop."

"Thanks, W.B.," she said sarcastically. "And you wonder why I think you're only *shirt* smart . . ."

"You thought her pie was bad? Really? I thought it was delicious," Deputy Buddy said, looking quite surprised. "In fact, it's quite possibly the best pie I've ever tasted."

Rose blushed again as she fluttered her eyelashes at the deputy.

"You're very sweet," she said.

"He may be sweet, but your pie wasn't," I insisted. "In fact, every pie you've ever baked has tasted sourer than a rotten lemon. There's nothing sweet about your pies other than the sweet relief you feel after spitting them out."

"Do you have a point, W.B., or do you just enjoy insulting me?"

"I . . ."

Wait, did I have a point?

Oh, that's right.

Yes. Yes, I did.

"You couldn't possibly have baked the winning pie," I told her. "And you know it. Someone must have used the Doppelgänger Device on you as well, and posed as you at the Pitchfork Fair, before entering the exploding pie in the contest. I was wondering why I saw you at the fair dressed in two separate outfits, first in your regular clothes, and then in your stupid looking dress and funny clown makeup . . ."

I trailed off as I realized that Rose was still wearing her stupid looking dress and clown makeup. I coughed into my fist and looked down at my shoes, hoping that she hadn't heard the last thing I'd said.

She had.

"First of all, W.B., Buddy happens to think my dress

and hair and makeup look nice. And secondly, why didn't you say something earlier about seeing me dressed in two different outfits at the fair?"

"Well, I was a little bit distracted."

"By what?" she asked as her brow furrowed. "By pie? You were distracted by pie again, weren't you? You're always distracted by pie."

She was right.

"I don't remember," I lied. "But I'm sure that someone else must have seen you dressed in two different outfits as well. That should be enough to set her free, right Deputy Buddy?"

Deputy Buddy frowned.

"I'm afraid not, kid. My dad will need more proof than that. He's pretty upset right now. He really loved that pen."

The three of us sat there and tried our best to think of a solution, when suddenly Rose had a brain sneeze of her own.

"Idea!" she cried out as she jumped, then flushed with embarrassment. "Umm, excuse me. I don't know what came over me. What about the baking contest sign-in sheet from the fair? Every person who entered a pie, tart, or cake into the contest needed to sign the sign-in sheet, which gave them an entry number and a place to put their dessert on the table. If W.B. is right, and another person showed up pretending to be me, then my name will appear on the sign-in sheet twice! And it will also show which one of us baked the exploding pie!"

"That's brilliant, Rose!" I cried, and then I started to do our family happy dance.

I was about three seconds into the happy dance before Deputy Buddy came up behind me, and began to slap me on the back as hard as he could.

"What are you doing?" I gasped as I flopped onto the floor.

His face turned bright red.

"Oh. Sorry, kid. I thought you were choking."

A few hours later, Deputy Buddy Graham returned to the jailhouse. He was panting and sweaty as he wiped his face with his handkerchief. He had left the jailhouse to look for answers, specifically the answer to what had happened to the sign-in sheet from the Pitchfork Fair.

While the person who had posed as Rose had stolen her face and her voice with the help of my parents' invention, they likely hadn't studied her well enough to perfectly copy her signature. All that we had to do was compare the two signatures, and we'd be able to spot the fake. That might not be enough evidence to make the rest of the town believe that she was innocent (the people in Pitchfork were famous for the grudges they held. In fact they still held a terrible grudge against England—not for the Revolutionary War from over a hundred years ago, but because they found it terribly confusing that the English referred to cookies as biscuits. "What in tarnation do they call biscuits then? Kumquats?" a typical Pitchfork townsperson would ask with a sneer), but hopefully it would be enough to convince Sheriff Graham to release Rose. We figured that everyone else would be convinced once my parents realized that their invention had been used for evil, and then gave the entire town a demonstration of what a villain could do with the Doppelgänger Device.

"Well, I have good news, and I have bad news, and I have some news that's neither good nor bad," Buddy said. "Which would you like to hear first?"

"Good news!" cried Rose.

"News that's neither good nor bad!" I cried.

Buddy ignored me and spoke to Rose.

"The good news, is that I know where the baking contest sign-in sheet is. It wasn't destroyed, so there is evidence that someone entered a pie while pretending to be you."

Rose and I cheered. I started to do the happy dance again, but stopped when I saw Rose quickly shake her head. Apparently, she wasn't willing to do the family happy dance in front of her new friend. Like I said, it can be rather embarrassing. I used to find it humiliating when my parents would do it in front of other people, but then I realized that being happy and joyful was more important than what other people thought.

I was about to comment on this, when I happened to notice that Deputy Buddy was smiling doofily at Rose. And she was smiling doofily back at him. In fact, they both kept making doofy faces at each other, and I began to wonder if something was going on that I wasn't aware of. Like maybe a gas leak.

"So what's the bad news?" she asked.

Deputy Graham's doofy grin was quickly replaced by a frown (which was still pretty doofy looking).

"The bad news," he said, ". . . is that it's at the Pitchfork Desert Dump."

"Oh."

"Oh."

"Yeah."

That wasn't bad news. That was *very* bad news.

The Pitchfork Desert Dump was where all the garbage from town was shipped. It was a large, fenced-in part of the desert located in Northern Arizona Territory. Once a month, the town would pay people to pack up carriages filled to the brim with the town's trash, and travel up north to drop it off at the dump. I had never been there before, but I'd heard it was one of the foulest places on the planet. There were rumored to be at least a thousand rats living there, rats that had formed their own rat town, known as Ratville, with their own rat mayor, rat sheriff, rat deputies, rat criminals, and even a little rat tailor to sew all their little rat clothes. That was probably just a schoolhouse story, but you have to admit it's a pretty cute one. Maybe people wouldn't find rats as gross if rats simply wore pants.

It would only take a few hours to reach the dump on horseback, but the real trouble started once you got there. According to the father of one of my classmates, the dump was completely unorganized. The people who were paid to haul the trash up there would simply toss it wherever there was room, sign their names to the dump record book, and then turn around and come back home. Garbage from yesterday would be mixed in with garbage from ten years ago, so no one knew where anything was.

There were also people who regularly traveled to the

dump in order to rummage through the trash in search of things to sell, making an even bigger mess. My father used to enjoy driving his horseless carriage up to the dump to search for parts that he could use for his inventions, until one day he brought home a large cushioned chair that had a family of raccoons living inside. The raccoons were very kind to my father, however they hissed at my mother, scratched up the furniture, made terrible messes in the kitchen, and one of them managed to lock Aunt Dorcas outside while she was wearing only her bloomers. Ever since then, my mother had forbidden him to pick up anything from the dump. She had also forbidden raccoons from coming into the house, though my father would still try to sneak one in from time to time.

I asked Buddy if he knew who had taken the trash up to the dump last. If they could remember where they had left the most recent collection of garbage, maybe it wouldn't be quite as difficult to find.

Buddy's face turned even redder than his hair.

"Actually," he said in a quiet voice, "I was one of the people who took the last batch of trash to the dump. And I can't remember where we put it. I can't imagine any of us would. Everything sort of looks the same up there, just really dirty, and smelly, and . . . dumpy."

I could tell by the look on Rose's face that she was incredibly disappointed. She was trying to stay calm, but it must have been upsetting for her to know that she might be locked up in jail for good, with no one but a sleeping deputy, doofy Buddy Graham, and a few mice to keep her company.

"But," Deputy Buddy said quickly, "that doesn't mean that I won't try! I'm going to go to the dump right now and find that piece of paper! I don't care if it takes me all year to find it! I don't care if I have to dig through every bag of trash that's up there. I'll find it, and clear your good name, Rose. I promise."

"Thank you, Buddy," said Rose with a grin. "I know that you will. I have faith in you. Everything's going to be alright. We're going to beat this. We're going to show everyone the truth. And don't you dare do that stupid dance, W.B."

"Well, look who's too good for the happy dance all of a sudden . . ." I muttered.

Deputy Buddy grabbed his hat and rushed to the door, but before he could step outside, Rose called out to him.

"Buddy!"

He turned around and looked at Rose, his eyes shining in a funny sort of way that almost looked like tears. I looked at Rose and saw that her eyes were shining too.

As I've said before, I'm no detective, but I could tell that something strange was going on between them, and I was going to get to the bottom of it. Maybe they both had the same thing for lunch, and it was making them sick.

But then my stomach rumbled, and I thought of pie, and I forgot all about Rose and Buddy's doofy looks.

See, that's why I rarely get to the bottom of things. Because of pie.

"Yes, Rose?" Buddy said. "What is it?"

"Please be careful."

That seemed like a silly thing for her to say, considering the circumstances. Buddy was going to the Pitchfork Desert Dump to search for a piece of paper, not to fight a group of armed bandits. The worse thing he'd encounter up there would be all of those rats—though come to think of it, his famous father Sheriff Graham regularly had tough battles with skunks—battles which he always seemed to lose. If Buddy was as good a peace officer as his father, then maybe he would need a bit of luck, especially if the rats of Ratville were organized in their attacks.

"I'm always careful," Buddy told her with a grin, before taking a step forward and walking right into the wall beside the open doorway.

As he burned with embarrassment and rubbed his sore nose, I suddenly remembered that he had a third piece of news for us.

"What? Oh, you mean the news that isn't really good or bad?" Buddy asked when I brought it up. "Well, the people who used to volunteer to deliver all of the town's trash to the dump have refused to do it anymore, because the smell up there is now so terrible. Mayor Thornberry said he would be willing to pay me double to haul the trash up there on my own. So I guess it's good that I'll be making some extra money, though it's not so good that I'll have to take at least two baths afterwards to get the stink off me."

"Is it really worth it?" Rose said as she made a face.

Buddy shrugged.

"It's not that bad. Last time, I just put a clothespin over my nose while I dumped the trash and signed the record books, and then I quickly rode back home. I only passed out once or twice while I was there."

Wait a minute. Records? A new and terrible smell? *Brain sneeze!*

"Idea!"

Buddy's final piece of news didn't sound particularly interesting to Rose, but I found it to be *very* interesting, and also very useful. My brain had made a connection, and then it came up with ideas for proving both that Rose was innocent of her crimes, and also that I was the real W.B.!

I wasn't certain that my ideas would work, but I had to take a chance on them. Otherwise, I'd probably end up starving on the streets.

In fact, I already felt as though I was starving.

I was so hungry that I was getting dizzy.

I couldn't remember the last time I'd felt so hungry.

It seemed as though I hadn't eaten in weeks, maybe even months . . .

"Buddy?" Rose said slowly. "Before you leave, can you please take W.B. to your house and give him something to eat? He's staring at his hand as though it's a ham sandwich."

I Keep an Egg in My Closet, and You'll Never Guess Why

I had a plan.

My favorite part of a plan has always been the end part. And by "the end part," I mean when the plan has already been completed, and it turned out to be a wonderful success.

My least favorite part of a plan is the part where you actually have to do it. I wish that I could just skip that part, so I could get right to the part where you're sitting around a table with your friends, toasting each other with ice cream, and patting each other on the back for a job well done.

But unfortunately, life doesn't work that way. It doesn't allow you to skip the unpleasant parts and go right to the parts with ice cream. I don't know why. If someone had asked me to design life, I would have made it without all of the pesky problems and obstacles and troubles, and I would have added a lot of extra time for ice cream and naps. But unfortunately, no one bothered to ask me.

I had mentioned all of that to Rose a few weeks earlier, and she told me that I was the laziest person she'd ever met. And if I hadn't been so sleepy from the three servings of ice cream I'd eaten that day, I would have given her a piece of my mind.

After I had gone to Buddy's house, taken a bath, and had a large bowl of beef stew, he loaned me a clean pair of clothes to wear, and then he headed to the Pitchfork Desert Dump to search for the lost sign-in sheet.

He was also kind enough to let me have the last of the fried chicken and chocolate cake he had stored in his cupboard.

Well, to be perfectly honest, he didn't exactly *tell* me that I could have the chicken and cake, not with his *actual* words. But his body language spoke louder than his words, and when he tipped his cap to me and told me to lock up when I was done, I could tell what he really meant was, *"and if you really want some cake and fried chicken, W.B. my good friend, then gosh darn it, I think you should eat whatever's left in my cupboard."*

Life is much better when you listen to people's body language instead of just their words. And Rose says I'm not *people* smart . . .

I crept carefully over the sand dunes of the Pitchfork Desert until I spotted the Baron Estate. It looked just like it normally did. Very Baron-y and Estate-y. My family was probably inside eating lunch. M, P, Aunt Dorcas, and little W.B., all seated around the table in the kitchen.

How I hated that little W.B., that chubby faker with his terrible haircut and impressive horseback riding skills. I couldn't wait to expose him for the fraud he was. And then M and P would feel terrible about chasing me with brooms and pots and spoons.

The clothes that Buddy Graham had lent me were all much too large. I had to roll up the shirt sleeves and pant legs, and use a length of rope as a belt to keep the trousers from falling to the ground. But they were all light brown, which was a perfect color for sneaking around the desert. I actually covered myself in sticky sap and rolled around in the sand in order to fully blend in with my surroundings. It didn't feel particularly good, and I also ended up with some bugs and lizards stuck to me as well, but it was a great way to camouflage myself. My parents were very clever, and I was guessing that the person who was posing as me was quite clever too, so if I wanted to sneak into the Baron Estate, I was going to have to be clever as well. That way, I'd catch them all by surprise. And it would be a great surprise.

No one ever expects W.B. to be clever.

I crawled until I reached the white picket fence surrounding the Baron Estate. As I crawled, I took the time to appreciate the beauty of our home, which was surrounded by trees and greenery, even though it was in the middle of the dry and sandy Pitchfork Desert.

Several years ago, my mother had invented a special chemical that produced a practically endless supply of nutrients and moisture, which allowed us to grow things which otherwise wouldn't have survived a day in the dryness and heat. Like the lush trees and bushes, as well as the wide variety of fruits and vegetables growing in our garden. Our gardens were prettier and greener than all of the gardens we had visited as we traveled around the world, even the ones that received rain almost year round. It's funny how I never took the time to appreciate it before. Maybe there was an upside to a faker using my parents' invention to pose as me. It made me appreciate the little things in my life that I took for granted.

I crawled all the way to the row of green bushes surrounding the work garage, bushes which made for an excellent hiding place. I then peeked through the windows.

The work garage was empty. That probably meant my parents were still in the kitchen having lunch. I wondered what they were eating. Maybe I could sneak in there and quietly make myself a sandwich to give me energy, and while I was at it, I could swipe a piece of cake or two, and maybe a few—no! Food would have to come later. I had a job to do, and I needed to get my hands on the Doppelgänger Device as quickly as possible.

I crept around to the back door of the work garage and tried to open it.

It was locked. I frowned. My parents usually only locked their work garage at night, though if the fake W.B. had warned them that there was someone who'd been sneaking around the Baron Estate, then it would make sense for them to take extra precautions. In fact, I'd actually counted on them taking some extra precautions, which was why I knew exactly what I had to do next.

I had a Plan B. I'd never had a Plan B before. Normally

I just had a Plan A, and then if Plan A failed, I would run around screaming until everything sorted itself out. But not this time. This time, I was prepared.

I sat there, hidden in the bushes, and waited for the front door of the house to open. I knew that it would open soon. I checked the pocket-watch that Buddy had lent me (alright, he hadn't actually *said* that I could borrow it, but his *body language* told me that it would be fine), and as soon as the watch struck noon, the front door opened, and Aunt Dorcas stepped outside.

"Alright, everyone! I'm meeting Madge and the girls at the teashop! I'll be home in time for supper!" she called into the house, her shrill voice echoing like a dying bird falling from the sky. She shut the door and waddled her way down to the desert path leading to Pitchfork.

Aunt Dorcas always visited her friends at the teashop on Saturdays, Sundays, Mondays, and Wednesdays. It was something that I could always count on, like the sun rising, the earth turning, and my stomach rumbling. It was because of how predictable my aunt was that I'd been able to successfully come up with a Plan B for breaking into the Baron Estate.

I crawled around to the other side of the house and picked up the bucket beside our well. There was still water in the bucket, which I used to quickly wash the sand from my face and hair, and also to unstick the lizard that had been stuck to my head—that lizard had been a really good sport about the whole thing. I gave it a couple of crumbs as a thank you.

Once I was clean, I tiptoed over to the large tree beside the house and began to climb it as quietly as I could.

Now, you might be surprised to learn that I had yet to trip or fall or bump my head or even stub my toe as I quietly made my way around the Baron Estate. I was pretty surprised about that myself. It could have been the record for the longest I had gone without stumbling or hurting myself, or, at the very least, without knocking over something valuable and breaking it.

And because that thought suddenly occurred to me as I was climbing, I had my first major slip up.

I had climbed the tree trunk and was slowly inching across a branch that led to Aunt Dorcas's open window, when suddenly my shirt sleeve got caught. It hooked on a splintered branch underneath my arm, and I couldn't seem to shake myself free.

The shirt that Deputy Buddy Graham let me borrow came down to my knees, and the sleeves were so long that I had to roll them up so I wouldn't look ridiculous. But as I tried to get my sleeve free from the branch, the other sleeve came unrolled, and suddenly the cuff was hanging six inches over my hand. I couldn't free my caught sleeve, and I also couldn't roll up my other sleeve, no matter how hard I tried, so I got frustrated and decided just to pull off the whole stupid shirt and let it fall to the ground. It landed in the well, which meant it was gone for good. I suppose I'm not that *shirt smart* after all.

I'm sure Deputy Buddy would forgive me for losing his clothing, though.

His body language told me he would.

I carefully crawled across the branch until I reached its end. Aunt Dorcas's bedroom window was wide open, and the end of the branch was only about three feet away from it. Three feet might not sound like much to you, but when you have to jump three feet from a tree branch into a second story window, where if you fell you had nothing to cushion you except for some rocks and a bunch of thorny rose bushes, then it seemed like a pretty darn long distance to jump. But I didn't have any choice. It was the only way I could sneak inside. I felt my nerves bubbling in my belly as I prepared to spring like a frog, or a toad, or a . . . well . . . a spring. After taking a deep breath, I dove off the tree branch with my arms outstretched.

I caught the windowsill with my fingertips. I tried to pull myself up and into the window, but it appeared as though I had exhausted my arm strength for the moment, so instead I just hung there like an out-of-shape bat.

As I hung, I felt something tickling my midsection. I looked down just in time to see the rope belt that I'd fashioned come undone, and the next thing I knew, Deputy Buddy's trousers had fallen into the rose bushes below. I probably wouldn't be able to remove them from the thorny bushes without ripping a few holes in them.

That meant I owed Buddy yet another apology. I was beginning to lose track of all the apologies I owed him. Maybe I could just give him one giant apology to cover all of the things that I'd done, as well as the things I'd probably do in the future.

Hanging from my aunt's window, dressed in nothing but my long johns and boots, I gritted my teeth and used every bit of strength I could find to pull myself up and into Aunt Dorcas's bedroom. I landed rather clumsily (as usual), but I didn't think I'd made too much noise until I heard my mother call from downstairs.

"Dorcas? Is that you up there? I thought you were going out!"

I sat there and held my breath. My brilliant idea had

been to sneak into Dorcas's room while she was gone, and then wait there until I knew the coast would be clear. Then I could sneak downstairs, slip into the work garage, find the Doppelgänger Device, and use it to prove to my parents that I was the real W.B.

But if my parents already knew that someone was in the house, and they assumed that it was only Dorcas (because frankly, she's always yelling and crying and shrieking and singing and yodeling and moaning, sometimes all at the same time—so we often don't listen to her when she tells us things, like that she's going out, or that she can't find her ear medicine), so why didn't I just pretend to be Dorcas?

I'd done it once before, and my imitation of her had been good enough to fool Rose Blackwood. Remember how I said that it was easy to act like W.B.? Well, it's even easier to act like Aunt Dorcas. You just need to be very weepy and loud, and wear the sort of clothing that makes you feel as though you're more of a pillow than a person.

I opened her closet and pulled out one of her poofier dresses and one of her fluffier bonnets, since they would cover most of my body, and therefore make the best disguise. As I dug through her closet, I paused when I discovered something on the closet floor, beside her collection of uniquely ugly and bafflingly uncomfortable boots.

It was a single egg.[1]

It was just sitting there, minding its own business, just like any other polite little egg in a closet. I stared at it for a moment, before shaking my head.

After slipping on a pair of her glasses, frilly gloves, and lacing up her complicated and unnecessarily pointy boots, I used a powder puff to powder my face so it would be as pale as Aunt Dorcas's.

That, as it turned out, was a horrible mistake. I must have been seriously allergic to the powder, which meant that I couldn't stop sneezing, and every time I sneezed, my aunt's very tight and very uncomfortable boots felt as though they were squeezing my feet in a vice grip, so I would shriek.

As I left Aunt Dorcas's room, with every few steps I took, I sneezed and shrieked.

"AH-CHOO—EEEEEEEEP!"

I began to panic as I made my way down the stairs, wishing that I had skipped the powder. I was drawing more and more attention to myself, which was the dumbest

---

1. In case you're curious, that is a mystery that has remained a mystery. My eggy aunt keeps a single hardboiled egg in her closet. And no one knows why.

The world can be a very confusing place sometimes, don't you think?

thing a person could do while sneaking around their parents' home while dressed as their aunt. I might as well have been stomping up and down the stairs and shouting, "Hey! There's a sneaking person sneaking around here! And it's me! I'm the sneaker! Just sneaking about sneakily! Call me Sneakers McSneakyboots!"

But as it turned out, putting on the powder was an unintentional stroke of genius. My aunt had been battling terrible allergies due to the all the plants blooming in M's garden, and she was always shrieking about something or other. So as I shuffled through the house while sneezing and shrieking, my parents and W.B. simply ignored me, just like they would have if I were the real Aunt Dorcas. They didn't even look up from their lunch, which I saw was red beans and rice, which happened to be one of my all-time favorite lunches. It smelled heavenly. I thought to myself that perhaps I could just sneak a little bowl or two, with some sour cream, and maybe some garlic bread as well, and was that a pie cooling on the window sill? Boy, that pie would sure taste good with some ice cream and—

NO!

I would not allow myself to grow distracted by pie. Again. There would be plenty of time for pie and red beans and rice and garlic toast and . . . you know what? I'm not going to go into detail about the food anymore.

While continuing my sneezes and shrieks, I made my way past the kitchen where P was telling M about a problem he was having with another one of their old inventions. "W.B." was reading one of his adventure books.

Silly W.B. His nose was always stuck in a book. No wonder he never had any idea what was going on. I cackled quietly to myself as I walked past him. What a fool.

Without making a sound (other than the sneezes and shrieks), I opened the side door and slipped into the work garage. My mother was typically a very organized person, but P was not, which meant that the work garage was a half-organized, half-unorganized work space. That worked just fine for them, but it could make things a bit tricky for people who were snooping around the work space and looking for a particular invention that could save them from an evil impostor.

Opening cabinets and drawers at random, searching through the stacks of metal and brass and wooden devices piled on top of the work bench, I struggled as I tried to remember exactly what the Doppelgänger Device had looked like. I remembered it was sort of bread-like in shape, with a lot of copper piping around it. There were two buttons on it, one which copied a person, and the other which transformed you into the person who was copied. As I sorted through all of their mysterious devices, I had a rare moment of wishing that I'd paid attention to my parents when they were describing their inventions. That would have made everything much easier.

I found three different devices that could have been the Doppelgänger Device. I laid them out on the work-bench and stared at them. They were all a similar color, made from similar gears and springs, with two buttons on either side. In the center of each was a little glass piece that looked as though it belonged on one of P's microscopes. I looked through all three of the glass pieces, and saw little numbers and letters and funny symbols. People with brains like M and P could look at those numbers, letters, and symbols and somehow make sense of them. I looked at them and saw a homework assignment from Miss Dan-ielle, which I would have to lie about and pretend was eaten by our dog.

(I know this has nothing to do with the story, but I often I wondered if Miss Danielle believed me when I told her that my homework was eaten by our dog. With all of the strange things that happened around the Baron Estate, a homework-eating pet would likely be considered one of my simpler and more believable stories. I mean, I've flown across the country in a house, for goodness' sake. I've walked across the ocean floor in an underwater breathing suit. It would be really silly of my teacher not to believe that my homework assignment was eaten by our dog, which was the sort of thing that happened all the time.

In fact, if my family actually had a dog, I think I would have been insulted by her doubts.)

Anyway, I had no choice but to test all three inventions, one by one, until I discovered which one was the Doppelgänger Device.

I picked up the first invention, pointed it at a bucket in the corner of the work garage, and pressed one of the buttons. The device made a weird belching noise as it spat out a beam of light, which I assumed meant that it was copying the bucket. Then I pointed the device at a broom and pressed the other button, expecting the broom to transform into a perfect copy of the bucket.

It did not.

After it was hit by the beam, the broom began to shake and spin like a tornado, bouncing up and down as it was bathed in a twinkle of mysterious light. Suddenly, the broom sprouted wooden arms and legs from its handle, arms and legs which began to move as though the broom had somehow come to life. I stared in wonder as the broom walked up to me, and used its bristles to brush my face as though it was saying hello.

I whispered "*hello,*" back to the broom and reached out to shake its wooden hand.

I must have done or said something that was considered very offensive to brooms, because then it tried to kill me.

The angry broom chased me all over the work garage, as I tripped and stumbled and sneezed and shrieked. And I'm certain that I would have been pummeled to death by those little wooden fists if I hadn't grabbed P's axe from his work bench, and chopped the murderous broom into splintery bits. I breathed a sigh of relief, and then sneezed a sneeze of relief, as I wiped my sweaty forehead with Aunt Dorcas's sleeve.

I was about to try the next device, when suddenly I heard a series of little scritches and scratches coming from behind me.

I turned around and saw that the chopped bits of the broom had formed into thousands of tiny little brooms, which attacked me again as though they were a tiny broom army! They climbed me like a tree and continued to punch me—though their fists were too small to actually hurt me, it was still very annoying. I found a big bucket of glue beneath the work bench, and after brushing the tiny brooms off me, I poured the glue over them. Once they were stuck together, I dropped a blanket over the whole gluey mess and kicked it underneath the workbench. I could hear the broom bits continue to struggle to unstick themselves and grumbling even though they didn't have mouths. Splinters don't give up easily.

After pausing for a moment to think about the truly mad things that happened in my parents' work garage, I attempted to use the second invention to see if it was the Doppelgänger Device.

This time, I tried to point the device at something smaller and softer than a broomstick, so in case it came to life and attacked me, it wouldn't hurt quite as much. I pointed the device at some sawdust and pressed a button to copy it. Then I pointed it at a rag, feeling quite confident that, if push came to shove, I could easily beat up a rag. I pressed the second button and a rainbow-colored light shot out of the end of the device.

The rag stirred, and then slowly began to float in the air, twisting and wrinkling itself until it had formed what looked to be a mouth. The mouth began to move, making noises as though it was clearing its throat (even though it didn't have a throat), and then it began to sing.

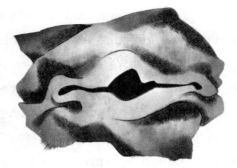

"*The Camptown ladies sing this song, doo-dah! Doo-dah! The Camptown racetrack's five miles long! Oh de doo-dah-dey!*"

"Oh, come on . . . seriously?" I groaned, feeling so sick of that song that I could live to be a thousand and never want to hear it again.

My father must have invented the weird singing device back when we still enjoyed hearing "Camptown Races."I really wished that he wouldn't use his talents for inventing this sort of nonsense. In fact, I'd rather he invent terrible things like Lefty and Lefty Also's "Indoor Outhouse."That invention sounded disgusting but nowhere near as annoying as this.

I grabbed the rag and tried to shush it, using both of my hands to cover its mouth, but the rag kept on singing. Its powerful voice tickled my palms. I began to worry that someone inside would hear it. If all of the screaming and wood chopping hadn't made them curious about what was going on in the work garage, then certainly the loud and obnoxious singing would. I was forced to do something drastic.

I went to the coal stove in the corner, opened it up to make sure it was burning, and then threw the rag inside.

"*Oh de doo-dah-aaaaaaaaaaaaaaauuuuuuughhhhhhhhhhhh!*"

And then it was silent. I closed the stove.

Feeling very pleased with myself for my quick thinking, I turned back towards the workbench, and spotted something very unpleasant.

There was another person in the garage.

It was W.B. He was standing in the doorway, and he had a gun in his hand. I'd never seen W.B. with a gun in his hand before. It looked about as unnatural as a duck carrying an abacus. I wondered if he'd ever used it before (W.B. with the gun, not the duck with the abacus, I mean). I sort of hoped that he hadn't, but then again, I sort of hoped that he had. W.B. wasn't the sort of person you wanted pointing a gun at you if he wasn't familiar with guns. That klutz could really do some accidental damage if he wasn't careful. Just between you and me, he really isn't the sharpest spoon in the drawer.

"Hello, *Aunt Dorcas*," W.B. said in a soft but dangerous voice. "Do you have something that you'd like to tell me?"

"Yes," I said, trying my best to keep my voice from shaking. "I keep an egg in my closet, and you'll never guess why."

THEN I LOOKED AT MYSELF AND WE BOTH FROWNED

W.B. pressed the gun to my back and led me out the back door of the work garage.

"Where are we going?" I asked.

"Be quiet," W.B. grunted back.

"Okay," I whispered. "Where are we going?"

"I didn't mean whisper. I meant *don't talk*."

"Then you should have said *don't talk*."

"Don't tell me what I should say!" W.B. hissed at me. "I have a gun!"

"Typical W.B.," I said as I rolled my eyes. "You can't even take a bit of constructive criticism without having a hissy fit."

W.B. whacked me on back of the head with the handle

of his pistol. It didn't hurt because I was still wearing Aunt Dorcas's big puffy bonnet, but I pretended that it did so W.B. wouldn't do it again. That guy is pretty easy to fool sometimes.

"Shut up!" W.B. said as he led me into the desert. "And keep walking until I tell you to stop."

I was a bit worried because he wasn't leading me down the normal path that went from the Baron Estate to Downtown Pitchfork. In fact, we weren't traveling on any sort of path at all. It seemed as though we were simply walking in a random direction into the desert, hiking across the sand, climbing over dunes, which is not very easy to do while dressed in your aunt's pointed boots and largest dress. I tried to explain this to W.B., but he wasn't very sympathetic.

"That's not my fault," he said. "I didn't tell you to dress up like your aunt."

We kept heading south until we reached a part of the desert that I was certain I'd never been to before. It was where the desert landscape was interrupted by the edge of a tall cliff.

I stared over the edge of the cliff, which had a dramatic slant. Several tiny pebbles rolled down the slant, picking up speed as they bounced, before dropping several hundred feet to the ground. The cliff overlooked a large, rocky valley, with no town or people or anything else for miles. It was a very long way to the bottom. As we stood there near the edge, with W.B. still pointing his gun into my back, I began to wonder what might happen next. Things didn't look too good for old W.B., and by "old W.B.," I meant me. Things were looking just fine for the other W.B. I sort of wished that I was the other W.B., with his impressive riding skills, as well the fact that he was the one with the gun.

"You just *had* to come back, didn't you?" said W.B. as he shook his head in disgust. "You wouldn't disappear quietly, would you? Well, you can't say that I didn't give you a chance. It didn't have to end this way."

"It still doesn't have to end this way," I told W.B. "Look, why don't you just go back to where you came from, and go back to being whoever it is that you actually are? Then I can go back to being me, and we can forget about this whole thing."

I thought it was a decent offer, and if I were W.B. (the other one, not me), I probably would have taken it. Yes, I'm a bit lazier than the average villain, but I like to think I'm a lot more sensible than the average villain as well. In all of the adventure stories I've read, the hero always ends up winning in the end, so if the villain would simply give up when he was given the chance, then he could avoid all of the unnecessary trouble.

"I don't think so," W.B. told me. "You see, I have a plan that can only succeed if there's only one W.B. around. And that W.B. has to be me. So you're going to have to disappear. For good, this time."

He glanced over to the slanted edge of the cliff. I glanced over towards the edge as well, and suddenly felt very dizzy. In fact, I became so dizzy that I started to fall. As I fell, I quickly reached out and grabbed W.B. to steady me.

That surprised W.B., who tried to push me off of him, but I had thrown him off balance as well, and soon we were both falling. We dropped in a clumsy heap and then the slanted ground caused us to roll towards the edge of the cliff. W.B. gasped as he reached out and caught an overturned tree to save himself from going over, dropping his gun in the process. The gun continued to tumble and roll over the side of the cliff, falling all the way to the bottom of the valley. We never heard it hit the ground.

I was still holding onto W.B. as tightly as I could, with my legs dangling helplessly over the edge of the cliff. Though I was exhausted and weak from a lifetime of being exhausted and weak, I needed to summon all of my strength in order to get myself out of that jam. W.B. groaned as I pulled myself up by using his legs, and then walked across his back and his head, making certain to squash his spine with the sharp heel of Aunt Dorcas's boots.

Served him right.

"How can you stand being in this body?" he moaned at me from the ground as I squashed him. "It's so useless and uncoordinated! I can't stop losing my balance!"

"Yeah, well, I've had to deal with it a lot longer than you have, so I don't have a lot of sympathy for you," I said, and then I turned and ran.

I had to get away, and I had to get away quickly. If I could reach the Baron Estate before W.B., then I could tell my parents about everything that had happened. I could warn them that the W.B. who they thought was me was actually an impostor, an evil stranger who was trying to get me out of the picture.

Unfortunately, Aunt Dorcas's dreadful dress and pointy boots struck again. I hadn't taken more than a half dozen steps before I tripped and fell in a tangle of poofy lace. I tried to untangle myself and stand so I could continue to make my getaway, but that lousy W.B. had caught up to me. He tore off one of the sleeves of my aunt's frilly dress and tried to use it to tie my hands behind my back.

"You tore my dress!" I yelled angrily, as I yanked my wrist from his grip. "Now *you'll* have to buy me a new one! And it had better be pretty!"

The funny thing about battling yourself is that it's really hard for you to get the upper hand. You're just as strong as yourself, so you can't really overpower you, no matter how hard you try. W.B. was grunting in frustration as I caught his wrist and tried to push him away.

"Stop fighting back, and let me kill you!" he ordered.

"No!"

"Why not?"

"Well, first of all, you didn't say please!"

We continued to wrestle each other, with W.B. getting me in a headlock, me elbowing him in the stomach, him smashing my head into a cactus, me throwing a handful of sand into his eyes to blind him, him stuffing pebbles up my nose to congest me, me jamming a tumbleweed into his ear because no one likes a tumbleweed in the ear, until soon we were both completely covered in sand, sweat, and bruises.

W.B. poked me in the eye, which he knew I hated, and so I responded by sitting on his head, which I knew I hated as well. He wrapped the torn sleeve of Aunt Dorcas's dress around my neck and tried to strangle me, so I pulled on his suspenders and let go so they would thwack him hard against the chest. We grabbed each other's noses and began to pull, both of us whooping as we dropped to the ground and spun around, pulling and whooping and spinning like a crazy propeller made of angry ferrets.

"Nyyyaaaaahhhhhh!" we both cried through our pulled noses.

We wanted to keep fighting, but the desert sun was really beating down on us, and slowly stealing our energy. Even in the wintertime, a sunny afternoon in the Pitchfork Desert can have you sweating like a pig in a fur coat, especially if you aren't in the shade. We were panting so heavily that we could barely speak.

"You're . . . you're so out of shape," W.B. gasped as he wiped the sweat from his eyes. "Oh my gosh, I feel like your heart's going to explode . . ."

I wanted to say something nasty back, but I couldn't speak, because quite frankly I felt the same way. My heart was pounding so loudly that it was beginning to give me a headache. W.B. and I lay there in the sand, desperately trying to catch my breath, when suddenly we heard the sound of footsteps. It sounded like a pair of people had randomly discovered us fighting in the desert. I sat up and attempted to wave to them, letting them know that I was the one who was in danger.

But it wasn't a pair of people. It was just a horse, my father's horse, Geoffrey, to be specific. Geoffrey whinnied and neighed as he looked from me, over to W.B., and then back to me again.

"It's me," W.B. said to the horse, still gasping for breath. "Get him."

I didn't understand why he would bother saying that to a horse, but then again, my father always told me that Geoffrey was much smarter than the average horse.

In fact, Geoffrey then proved how smart he was by trotting over to me, picking me up by gripping the back of my dress in his teeth, and then he began to carry me over to the edge of the cliff.

"Woah, Geoffrey, stop it!" I ordered as I tried to wiggle free. "That's a very bad horse!"

But my words had no effect on him. I managed to unbutton the back of Aunt Dorcas's dress and slipped out of it. Once my feet hit the sand, I started running, but W.B. and Geoffrey were after me in an instant. W.B. might have been as slow as me, but Geoffrey the horse wasn't, and before I knew it I was once again being led to the cliff's edge.

"Please, I'll give you carrots," I said to Geoffrey, trying to bribe him into taking my side. "All the carrots you could ever want. Oats too. And hay, and sugar cubes, and anything else you want. I'll even tell P to stop making those stupid hats for you."

Geoffrey paused for a moment, seriously considering the last part of my offer, before W.B. told him to quit his lollygagging. Together, they dragged me the rest of the way to the edge of the cliff. And perhaps they would have thrown me over, which would  have spelled the end for W.B. (the real one, which is me, in case you had forgotten), if we hadn't heard a familiar voice call out:

"Both of you get away from my horse! Geoffrey, come here!"

W.B. and I let go of one another. Geoffrey the horse bowed his head and immediately trotted over to my father, who was clearly in charge. As my father stared at us he pulled a small, snail-like item from his ear, which I recognized as his *Listen Up, Stephen* Device. He must have been wearing that device and heard us all the way out here in the desert.

I also noticed that P was also holding two other inventions. One of the inventions was the Doppelgänger Device. I didn't recognize the other one. My mother stood beside my father and clutched his arm tightly, a look of terror on her face.

"W.B.?" she said to us.

"Huh?" W.B. and I both replied. Then I looked at myself and we both frowned.

WEARING A HORSE'S SADDLE OVER HIS NETHERS

That brings us to the present, where P is trying to decide which one of us to use the Gänger-Doppel Device on.

"Wait, McLaron," said M. "Can't we just tie them both up for six to eight hours and wait? Eventually, the effects of the Doppelgänger Device will wear off, and we'll see who the real W.B. is."

P shook his head as he handed M the Doppelgänger Device.

"I'm sorry, Sharon," he said. "But I'm afraid that won't work. Someone with a clever mechanical mind has fiddled with the original Doppelgänger Device and made it so the effects will be permanent. Without using the

Gänger-Doppel Device to reverse the effects, we'll never know which one is really our son."

"That's where you're wrong!" a familiar and happy sounding voice called out.

We all turned and saw Shorty pull up to us in the horseless carriage. As she hopped out, she patted the buggy appreciatively on its side.

"That's a mighty fine invention, Mr. and Mrs. Baron," Shorty told my parents. "I can see why B.W. was so interested in stealing it from you."

"B.W.?" my mother frowned. "But we haven't seen him in a week. The poor dear is sick in bed with the Russian flu."

Shorty looked from W.B., to me, and then grinned.

"No, he's not," she said. "He's right here. I know for a fact that B.W. has been tinkering with your inventions without your permission. I've watched him sneak into your work garage and steal parts from your devices. And the last time I was here, I spied on him and watched him swipe three of your blueprints. One was the blueprint for this horseless carriage. The second was for a shield made of an invincible material. And the third was for your gun that actually builds bullets as it fires. I think he was planning on—"

"Putting the three inventions together so that the horseless carriage could become a vehicle used for war," P finished, a lightbulb of realization clicking on over his head.

"Or crime," M added. "You could use an invincible horseless carriage like that to rob any bank in the country."

Suddenly, I had a brain sneeze. But luckily, I was able to keep it to myself this time. Sometimes it is best *not* to tell people when you've had an idea, or when something clever occurs to you out of the blue. Always let people think you're a bit dimmer than you actually are. I live my life by that rule.

"B.W. wasn't a sweet kid," Shorty continued. "He was a criminal who was taking advantage of you. He needed to learn more from you, so you could help him build more terrible inventions meant for crime. He needed to keep stealing your blueprints and the parts from your devices. And once he learned about your Doppelgänger Device, he realized that he could pose as W.B. and continue stealing from you, without you ever suspecting him. I waited to tell you all about my suspicions because I wanted to know for sure what his evil plan was before I made the accusation. I finally put all of this together as my parents were heading to another clinic to get my father's lip sewn up properly—

the last clinic accidentally sewed it up backwards, so when he spoke, he sounded like he was speaking French with a mouthful of cheese."

"*Quel fromage*," P said as he shook his head.

"I ran all the way back to the hotel in Pitchfork and found W.B.'s note, and then decided to come looking for him," Shorty continued. "I got to the Baron Estate and found it empty, so I followed your tracks out here. And it's a good thing I did."

I realized that I hadn't declared that I was the real W.B. in a while.

"I'm the real W.B.!" I cried.

"No, I'm the real W.B.!" W.B. (B.W.) cried.

Rats. I really thought it would work that time.

(By the way, I know it's going to be really confusing, but I'm going to start referring to the other W.B—the fake W.B.—by his real name, which is B.W. And if you think *you're* confused by that, then you should get down on your knees and thank your lucky stars that you're not me—the real me, I mean. Because I guarantee you that I'm at least fifty times more confused than you are. In fact, I'd bet all the tulips in Tallahassee on it.)

"Alright, so we now know *who* the impostor is. But how will we figure out *which one* of these W.B.s is the impostor?" M asked Shorty.

Shorty walked over to me and B.W. She scrunched up her face and looked us both in the eye. B.W. and I stared back at her, not understanding what it was that she was looking for.

"We should ask them questions that only the real W.B. would know the answers to," she finally announced. "Alright, W.B.s, what is my father's real name?"

. . . Oh no.

I have a terrible memory. And B.W. knows that I have a terrible memory. We talked about it the first day that we met. Or was it the second day? The sixth day? Wait, what day is it today? I looked over at B.W. He looked over at me. We both shrugged our shoulders at the exact same time, and mumbled something that sounded like a combination between "Jasper" and "Sherman" and "Barold", even though I'm pretty sure that Barold isn't a real name. The point was, we didn't know Shorty's father's name, which I could tell annoyed my little friend.

"W.B. has a terrible memory," P told Shorty. "He certainly wouldn't remember something like that. We should ask him something that he would actually know. Oooh, I've got it! W.B.'s, what is the mathematical formula I used to give the Baron Estate the power of flight?"

He grinned at us and wiggled his eyebrows.

"Huh?" said B.W. and I at the same time.

It was a trick question. I didn't know the answer to that question, or to any question related to science and mathematics. And my former best friend *knew* that I didn't know any of that stuff either, which meant that he wouldn't attempt to answer any of the science questions asked by my father, even if he knew the answers. He certainly was a clever one, that B.W., clever and evil. Which was a dangerous combination. He was clever enough to know when to play dumb.

B.W. scratched his head in confusion.

"Don't scratch my head," I told him.

"Sorry," he replied. "I thought it was *my* head."

Well played, B.W., well played.

M stepped forward.

"Alright, W.B.s," she said. "Whichever one if you is my son will certainly know the answer to this question: what is your favorite food?"

"All of it," B.W. and I said.

"Except for spinach," we quickly added.

"Why do you have a problem with squirrels?" P asked.

"I don't want to talk about it," B.W. and I replied awkwardly.

"What's the loudest thing in the world?" M asked.

"Aunt Dorcas when she's yodeling in the bath," B.W. and I answered.

I looked at B.W. and realized that I had told him quite a lot about myself, and he obviously had a fantastic memory and a very clever mind. There likely wasn't much about my life that he didn't know about. That meant questioning us probably wouldn't work. My parents continued to try though, asking us W.B. related questions for another hour, until they finally accepted that it was hopeless.

"Well, I'm out of ideas," P finally said. "I give up. I guess we just have two W.B.'s now. Let's look on the bright side. Now we have a spare in case anything happens to one of them."

"No, we don't have two W.B.s," M told him angrily. "We have our son, and we have an evil little criminal who is posing as him. McLaron, please, think of a way to uncover the fake."

"Alright, my little muffin."

My father quickly slipped into his very weird looking thinking position. It was the position he needed to be in when he had to think hard about something. He crouched down, stuck his tongue out, and scrunched up his face until he looked like someone who was suffering from both an upset stomach and a hideous rash.

Normally, my father would go into his thinking position, and a few moments later he would come up with a brilliant idea that would save the day.

But not this time.

Before he could think of what to do next, Shorty jumped six feet up in the air and shouted.

"Idea!"

When she landed, her face turned beet red.

"Sorry about that," she said sheepishly. "I don't know what came over me."

I did. Brain sneezes. They happen more often than you think.

"What is it, Shorty?"

"I know how we can prove which kid is the real W.B.," she said, walking over to Geoffrey the horse and taking his reins. "I want each of them to hop onto Geoffrey and ride him around in a circle."

B.W. and I looked at each other and frowned.

"I don't get it," I said.

"Yeah, what's that supposed to prove?" B.W. asked.

Shorty grinned mysteriously.

"You'll see. Which one of you would like to go first?"

B.W. raised his hand. Shorty motioned for him to get on the horse, which he did.

As he rode the horse in a circle, I could see him swaying uncomfortably on the saddle, as though he was about to fall off at any moment. When he was finished riding, he hopped off the horse and landed flat on his face. My parents exchanged curious glances.

Shorty helped B.W. up, and then motioned for me to climb onto the horse next, which I did.

Sort of.

As I pulled myself onto Geoffrey, I somehow managed to slide underneath his saddle instead of on top of it, and I got stuck. As I struggled to free myself, Geoffrey must have thought that I wanted him to start riding in a circle, which he did. My arms and legs were flailing as I tried to free myself, and I accidentally kicked the horse in the backside, causing him to buck and whinny, and then to run. As Geoffrey ran across the desert, I found myself getting more and more squashed by his saddle, which was squeezing me like an accordion. Finally, I managed to wiggle my way out of it, but when I did, I fell off the horse completely. One of Aunt Dorcas's bootlaces got caught in one of Geoffrey's horseshoes, so as the horse continued to gallop, it dragged me along, my head bouncing off every rock and scraping across every prickly cactus, until Geoffrey finally calmed down and trotted over to my parents.

Shorty ran up and untangled my bootlace from the horse, helped pick some of the cactus spikes from my eyes, and then grabbed the Gänger-Doppel Device from my father.

"This is the real W.B.," she announced as she pointed to me. "I'd bet all the tulips in Tallahassee on it."

She pointed the Gänger-Doppel Device at B.W. and pressed the button.

My mother and father held their breath and turned away, just in case they were about to witness their only son being turned inside out. A bright green light shot out of the Gänger-Doppel Device and hit B.W., transforming him back into himself.

"I never liked you," he growled at Shorty, once his true identity had been revealed.

"Really?" said Shorty with a frown. "But I always liked you."

"You did?"

"Hah! No. I always knew you were an evil little jerk! You tried to convince us to turn the real W.B. inside out, even though you'd still be exposed as an impostor!"

"Oh, come on!" B.W. snapped angrily. "Can the rest of you honestly say you've never been so frustrated with W.B. that you wanted to see something really terrible happen to him?"

Shorty opened her mouth to disagree, but then paused. M and P started to disagree as well, but then stopped and quietly cleared their throats instead. No one seemed to be in a hurry to defend good old W.B. In fact, everyone was trying really hard not to make eye contact with me.

"Seriously?" I said to my parents and my purported best friend. "You're siding with a murderous maniac over me?"

"I'm not a murderous maniac, you fool," B.W. replied as he rolled his eyes. "I was planning on escaping before anyone had to die. I knew that Mr. Baron would never use that device on either of us without knowing for certain who the real W.B. was. He can't even bring himself to kill a moth."

"That's because he's afraid of them," said M. "W.B. is too."

Shorty looked at me as though I was insane.

"You're scared of moths?" she asked.

"No, I just find it disturbing that they look like ghost butterflies. Shorty, quick! Lasso B.W. before he gets away!"

She whipped out the rope that she wore tied around her belt, and used it to quickly hogtie B.W.'s arms and legs before he could get away. As she did, M and P ran up to me and hugged me tightly.

"I'm so happy to have my son back," M said as she kissed me on top of the head.

"So am I," P told me. "Though I must warn you, you might not want to go around dressed in nothing but your long johns, son. I'm sure they're quite comfortable, but there are ladies present."

I picked up Aunt Dorcas's large dress from the ground. It was terribly stained and practically torn to shreds. I hoped she wouldn't be too upset about it—but then I remembered that it was Aunt Dorcas, which of course meant that she would be upset about it. I would try to make it up to her, though. Maybe I'd put another hard-boiled egg in her closet.

"Well, I suppose we can go home now," said M. "I'm sure the real W.B. must be starving."

She was right. The mere mention of food made my mouth water.

But before we went back to the Baron Estate, there was something I needed to show everyone first. It was what I had discovered when I had my brain sneeze earlier, the brain sneeze that I had held in by covering my brain nose and brain mouth with my brain hand.

It wasn't often that I knew something that no one else did, so I was going to take my time and enjoy explaining it to everyone.

"Before we go home," I announced, "I have something to show you all, which will most likely shock you. P, will you please look at the records within the Doppelgänger Device, the ones that tell you who the device has copied recently?"

P looked at M and shrugged his shoulders, before looking into the eyepiece in the center of the invention, and reading the strange and complicated equations that only made sense to a mind as strange and complicated as my father's.

"Hmmm . . . it says that the last three people the device was used to copy were W.B. and Rose Blackwood. Huh. And it recently copied someone else as well, though the device is having difficulty defining who that person is . . ."

"That's right!" I exclaimed. "The Doppelgänger Device was used on Rose so she would be blamed for the explosion at the Pitchfork Fair. B.W. had to get me out of the picture to continue his evil plan, but he also wanted to get Rose Blackwood out of the picture as well. He wanted her to go to jail for the rest of her life."

"Why would he want that?" M asked.

B.W. squirmed on the ground and grunted in annoyance.

"Because," I said as I took the Gänger-Doppel Device from Shorty, "he needed to have revenge."

"Revenge?" Shorty asked. "Why would B.W. need revenge against Rose? What did she ever do to him?"

"Absolutely nothing," I told her. "But she *did* do something terrible to his father. And his father is the one who's been helping him."

I heard B.W. groan from his place on the ground.

"I can't believe a dunce like you actually figured it out . . ." he muttered.

"His father?" M frowned. "Who is his father?"

I smiled.

"B.W.'s full name is Belford Eustace Nigel Egbert Doolittle Ignatius Cattermole Threepwood Whitestone."

"The Third," P added.

"His initials spell out BENEDICT. And his last name, Whitestone, sort of sounds like the opposite of—"

"Blackwood," M gasped. "His father is Benedict Blackwood!"

"How clever of you to figure that out, W.B.!" P cried, and then his smile faded as he stared at me suspiciously. "In fact, it sounds a bit *too* clever. Are we certain that you're the real W.B.?"

"But that's impossible," Shorty argued. "Benedict Blackwood is locked up in prison!"

I shook my head.

"He must have broken out of prison. In fact, I'll bet he used the Doppelgänger Device to transform himself into someone else, so he could sneak out of prison without anyone realizing he was gone! Is that true?" I asked B.W.

B.W. sighed as he nodded his head.

"Yes. I pointed the device at one of the deputies in the prison, and then I pointed it at my father. I switched their bodies, and then called the other deputies, and told them that Benedict had attacked the deputy. They locked up that deputy, and set my father free. It was a brilliant plan, and I would have gotten away with it, if it weren't for you, W.B."

"Where is Benedict Blackwood now?" P asked.

For a moment, B.W. didn't speak. He cleared his throat and looked up to the sky, as though he was thinking very carefully about his answer.

"Far, far away from here," he finally said, though it was easy to see that he was lying. "You'll never find him. And it doesn't matter if you lock me up in the world's most secure prison, my father will find a way to break me out. You can never beat Benedict Blackwood."

"Oh no?" I asked, pointing the Gänger-Doppel Device at Geoffrey.

"No, not my horse!" P shrieked. "You'll turn him inside out! Then it'll be impossible to brush his lovely hair!"

But it was too late. I had pressed the button. The green light shot out and hit the horse, which immediately transformed back into the person who he really was.

"Oh dear," said M as she quickly looked away.

"Yikes," said Shorty as she put her hat over her eyes.

It was Benedict Blackwood, wearing nothing but a horse's saddle over his nethers.

SOMETHING MUCH WORSE THAN "CAMPTOWN RACES"

Because I'm a gentleman, I handed Aunt Dorcas's torn dress to Benedict Blackwood, so he would have something to wear. He took it from me, and as he did, he reached out and grabbed the Gänger-Doppel Device as well.

"Hey!" I said, feeling like a fool as I stood there in my long johns. "I didn't tell you that you could have that!"

"I'm a criminal, you fool!" he snapped. "I do whatever I want to do!"

He slipped on the dress and pointed the Gänger-Doppel Device at us. We held up our hands in surrender, except for B.W., whose arms were still tied together.

"And now I'm going to get rid of you all, one by one,"

Benedict Blackwood told us as he placed his finger on the button of the Gänger-Doppel Device. "I just need to decide which one of you I'd like to shoot first . . ."

"Shoot them?" B.W. said with a frown. "Why do you need to shoot them?"

"Why do you care?" I asked him. "You were about to throw me off the edge of that cliff a few minutes ago."

"Yes, but I gave you a chance to live," B.W. told me. "Remember? I knocked you out and put you on that cross country train so I could get rid of you peacefully. I *didn't* want you to die. I was being nice."

"He's right, W.B.," M said.

"That actually was pretty kind of him," Shorty agreed. "I mean, it's probably as kind as a villain can be."

"You should be thanking B.W.," P told me.

"I'm not going to thank B.W.!"

"Son," Benedict Blackwood said as he turned to B.W. "I know you're new to this villain thing. But we aren't supposed to care about who we shoot. That's what makes us villainous. Understand? Nobody matters except for us."

B.W. shrugged.

"Fine," he said. "It just seems stupid to waste Mr. and Mrs. Baron's talents for inventing. They could be very useful to a brilliant criminal. Think of all the great inventions they could make for us."

Benedict thought about that for a moment.

"You're right," he said. "I could use those brainy fools to invent all sorts of great weapons for me. I'd be unstoppable. But I can shoot the other two, right?"

"Well . . ." B.W. said slowly. "You might not want to shoot Shorty either. I don't like her, but she's remarkably strong for her size. In fact, I've seen her make a grown man cry just by patting him on the back. With a bit of training, she could become a very useful member of your criminal gang. And no one would ever suspect her of being a villain. She could get away with anything."

"Good point," Benedict Blackwood agreed. "No one ever expects a cute little kid to be a villain. Alright, I won't shoot her either. But what about him?"

He pointed at me. B.W. looked at me and frowned. So did everyone else.

"Well, W.B. isn't particularly strong," B.W. began. "And he isn't particularly clever, or talented, or knowledgeable, or even very pleasant to be around. But . . . yeah, I suppose you can shoot him."

Benedict smiled as he pointed the Gänger-Doppel Device at me and started to press the button.

I winced and covered my face, peeking through my fingers and hoping that being turned inside out wouldn't be as painful as it sounded. And maybe there would be some benefits to being inside out. I wouldn't need to get haircuts anymore, for one thing.

Come to think of it, that would probably be the only benefit.

But before I could be hit by the green light from the device, the sound of a gunshot rang through the air. The Gänger-Doppel Device flew out of Benedict Blackwood's hands and landed several feet away.

"Good shot, Deputy Buddy!" M cried.

I looked over and saw Deputy Buddy Graham and Rose Blackwood on a pair of black horses. There was a smoking gun in Buddy's hands. The deputy shrugged sheepishly as he looked at my mother.

"Actually, it wasn't," he told her. "I was aiming for his head."

Several other deputies arrived and arrested Benedict Blackwood. As he was dragged away in chains, he screamed about how he was going to have his revenge on me and my family once and for all, which I suppose was meant to frighten us. But it was pretty hard to take him seriously while he was wearing Aunt Dorcas's ripped up dress. He certainly looked quite silly wearing it without the pointy boots, which were still on my feet. The boots completed the outfit.

My mother and father listened as I explained to them in detail how Rose was a victim of Benedict and B.W.'s evil plan. I told them that Benedict had posed as his sister and entered an exploding pie in the contest under her name.

"I should have known it was Benedict," Rose said as she shook her head. "Not only is he the evilest person I've ever met, he's also the most talented baker. The man would have been a first class pastry chef if he hadn't gone into crime. Any pie of his was bound to win first prize at the contest."

"But how did you prove Rose's innocence?" M asked Deputy Buddy. "You couldn't have known about the Doppelgänger Device, and how Benedict used it to pose as his sister."

"Did you find the sign-in sheet for the baking contest?" I asked him with a grin.

"Nope," Buddy said with a wink. "I found something

even more convincing. Little W.B. here told me that it would be almost impossible for me to find the sign-in sheet at the Pitchfork Desert Dump, so he suggested that I just pick up a few of Rose's old pies instead, the ones that she'd thrown away after baking them. They were quite easy to find. They were the stinkiest things at the dump."

"Oh, goodness," M said, her face turning a bit green. "You mean the rejected pies that smelled so awful that they made the wallpaper in the kitchen peel off?"

"Yup," said the deputy. "W.B. suggested I bring them down to the hospital and show them to my father. Pop took one look at them, and after throwing up his lunch, he realized that Rose couldn't possibly have baked that delicious pie. Woo-wee those pies smelled awful! They smelled like a gorilla's dirty underpants. Actually, they smelled worse than that. They smelled like if a sickly bat vom—"

"That's enough, Buddy," Rose interrupted crossly. "I think we all get the point."

"Right," Buddy said. "We realized that the real Rose had entered a pie in the contest that we'd mistaken for a disgusting joke. My father thought someone had put some goat plop in a pie tin for a laugh, but that was actually Rose Blackwood's entry. Once we figured that out, Pop declared that Rose should be freed from jail with a full apology."

"Speaking of apologies, Rose, can you ever forgive us for doubting you?" M asked. "We would love to have you come back and work for us again. We can't afford to pay you very much, but we can start giving you credit for some of the inventions and devices that you've helped us build. That means you'll get a percentage of everything we sell."

Rose's wide grin told her that she'd be thrilled to come back and work for my parents. And I was pretty thrilled about that too. Home hadn't felt quite like home without Rose. I missed having her at the Baron Estate.

Actually, home hadn't felt quite like home without *me* there either. I missed having me at the Baron Estate as well.

"Well, I don't think Rose will be worrying about money," said Deputy Graham. "She's offered to accompany me on the monthly trips to the Pitchfork Desert Dump to throw out the town's trash, and so I'm going to split the payment with her fifty/fifty."

"It looks like everything worked out quite well for all of you," B.W. said sourly. "How lovely. Now, can someone please untie me?"

"Oh, pipe down," said Shorty, as she stepped on his head. "You should be locked away in jail too. You tried to kill W.B."

"True," said B.W. "But I also kept my father from shooting all of you with that horrible invention. You'd all be inside out if it weren't for me."

M, P, and Shorty thought about that for a moment.

"I guess," said Shorty.

"I suppose that's true," M said with a nod.

"He did save us in the end," admitted P.

"That's right, I *did* save you," said B.W. "So please untie me. Everything can go back to the way it was before, just like you suggested earlier, W.B. I'll go back to my life, and you can go back to yours. Just give me what I deserve."

"What do you think, W.B.?" Rose asked. "You're the one who B.W. tried to kill. I think you should decide what happens to him."

Everyone seemed to think that was fair, even Buddy.

"Alright, we'll let the kid decide," said the deputy. "What should we do, W.B.? Should I arrest him, or should we set him free?"

I stared at B.W., who stared back at me blankly. I couldn't tell what he was thinking. He was much smarter than I was, which meant that this might have been some sort of trick. If I freed him, he might try to break his father out of prison, and then they would both come after me and have their revenge. After all, if he was clever enough to tinker with my parents' brilliant inventions, he could probably invent something pretty dastardly on his own.

But then again, he had saved my parents and Shorty from the Gänger-Doppel Device, and he tried to get me out of the way without hurting me, which meant that he probably wasn't *all* bad.

There had to be a way for me to repay him for saving us, but at the same time punish him for stealing my identity and then attempting to throw me off a cliff.

And then it hit me. A brain sneeze.

"Idea!"

"What are you doing?" B.W. cried, trying to free himself.

Shorty and I hoisted him up and into the train car. The train car was filled with bales of hay, and it smelled like animal plop, even though there weren't any animals in it. As far as train cars were concerned, this one didn't seem too bad, though I only had one other to compare it to.

"I'm just giving you what you deserve," I told my former best friend as we gave him another push, "that's all."

As B.W. rolled further into the train car, a couple of merry travelers poked their heads out. They'd been hiding in the shadows behind the hay bales, having snuck onto that particular train car without purchasing a ticket.

"Well, well, well," cackled Lefty Also. "If it ain't the funny looking kid from Texas! Good to see you, cowpoke! Hah hee!"

"Hah hee!" Lefty echoed.

"Hah hee!" I echoed as well. "Hi, Leftys. This is B.W. He'll be joining you on a cross-country trip."

"What?" said B.W., his eyes growing wide with panic. "No, I won't! Untie me! Untie me right now!"

I reached into my pocket and pulled out all of the money I'd made from dancing at the Pitchfork train station. It wasn't much, but to a pair of failed inventors who ate nothing but beans and crackers, it looked like a small fortune.

"Here you go," I said, as I handed Lefty and Lefty Also the money. "This is to repay you for your kindness, and also so you'll make sure that this kid doesn't get off the train until you've reached the East Coast."

"You got it, kid," said Lefty as he tipped his crushed hat at me. "We'll keep an eye on him like he's a porcupine at a nude beach."

"Umm, alright. Thanks. Anyway, have a nice trip, B.W.!"

The train conductor blew the whistle. The engine released a long string of steam, as the wheels began to turn, and the train started to chug along the tracks.

"I'll get you for this, W.B.!" B.W. shouted over the sound of the moving train. "I'll get you for this if it's the last thing I do!"

"Hey, Leftys!" I called. "Something I forgot to tell you! There's nothing B.W. loves more than a good song!"

"Huh?" said B.W.

The two Leftys laughed and slapped each other on the back as they stood. They both cleared their noses and throats, and then they started to sing.

"A-one, and a-two, and a-one-two-three . . . *the Camptown ladies sing this song, doo-dah! Doo-dah! The Camptown racetrack's five miles long! Oh de doo-dah-dey!*"

"Noooooooo!" screamed B.W. "Anything but that! Noooooooooooooo!!!"

My parents, Rose, Shorty, Deputy Buddy, and I all waved farewell to B.W. as the cross country train slowly carried him away.

"Nooooooooooooooooooooooooooooooooooooooooooooooo oooooooooooooooooooooooo . . ."

"Do you think that was too cruel?" I asked, when we

could no longer hear B.W.'s screams.

"He stole your identity," Shorty said.

"He tried to kill you," said M.

"He wanted to build deadly weapons to help his evil father," Rose said.

"His evil father whom he helped break out of jail," Deputy Buddy added.

"He tied up Geoffrey and hid him behind the barn for several weeks while his father posed as him," P said darkly. "In my opinion, you went too easy on him. If you hurt my son, you deserve to be punished. But if you hurt my horse, you deserve something much worse than 'Camptown Races.'"

EVERYTHING'S JUST HUNKY DORY

As I mentioned before, this is my favorite part of a plan: the part where the plan has already been completed, everything has turned out alright, and life can go back to the way it was before.

Well, life can *mostly* go back to the way it was before.

My parents ended up destroying both the Doppelgänger Device and the Gänger-Doppel Device. They realized it would be far too dangerous to have devices that could turn you into other people or turn other people inside out. We had seen firsthand what a criminal could do with an invention like that.

Several people from the government (we think they were from our government, though some of them spoke with weird accents and attempted to bribe us with money that had pictures of fish on it) came by and tried to convince my parents to build them Doppelgänger Devices as well, but they refused, no matter how much fish money they were offered. My parents would rather be poor than go against their morals.

Shorty's father finally met a doctor who convinced him to accept the fact that he would never grow a proper mustache. That might not sound like a big deal to you, and, frankly, it doesn't sound like that big a deal to me either. But, apparently, it was a big deal to Shorty and her mother.

They said it was a marvelous breakthrough, and they could finally have a life where they didn't have to worry about their father spending a fortune on fake hair tonic or catching fleas by repeatedly gluing animal tails to his upper lip. They packed up their things and headed back to Chicago.

"I don't suppose you could convince your folks to move out here?" I had asked Shorty as she and her parents boarded their train back home.

Since B.W. had turned out to be a villain, it meant that Shorty was once again my only friend. Though I had to admit, she was a pretty great friend to have. It was wonderful having someone in my life who I could trust, who I knew I could always count on.

"Maybe one day I will," Shorty told me with a big grin. "Or maybe you could convince your folks to move to Chicago. Either way, I'm sure I'll see you soon, Wide Butt."

And then she jumped up and kissed me.

I still have the bruise.

I no longer had a friend in school, but that didn't really matter. In my opinion, it was better to have no friends than to have a fake friend.

The other kids in school didn't seem to care that B.W. would no longer be their classmate, though Miss Danielle was pretty upset about it.

"But I had just learned how to say his name three times quickly," she groaned to me after she heard the news. "Belford Eustace Nigel Egbert Doolittle Ignatius Cattermole Threepwood Whitestone the Third, Belford Eustace Nigel Egbert Do—oh, what's the point?" she sighed.

"That's okay," I said as I patted her on the arm. "You can say his name to me as often as you like, Miss Danielle."

My teacher smiled.

"That's very sweet of you, Waldo."

I winced.

I actually think I prefer "Wide Butt" to "Waldo".

An uneventful month went by.

Then, one morning, Deputy Buddy Graham stopped by the Baron Estate. It was garbage day, the day that all of Pitchfork's trash had to be taken up to the Pitchfork Desert Dump.

Rose had dressed properly for the event, wearing her dingiest and dirtiest clothes, as well as a clothespin pinned over her nose. But I noticed she still painted her face in makeup and straightened her hair, which was strange for a trip to the dump. I mentioned that to M and Aunt Dorcas, and they both laughed and told me that I'd understand when I got older.

I hate when people tell me that. What if I don't understand when I get older? What if I understand *even less?* And how old are they expecting me to be before I understand? Thirteen? Fourteen? Eighty-six? If I had to be that old in order to understand, then I'd probably forget whatever it was that I'm supposed to be understanding in the first place.

"Rose? Buddy? Would you mind if we tagged along?" P asked, as they prepared to board the giant carriage filled with garbage. "Sharon and I are working on a new invention, and we're running a bit low on parts. Maybe we can find what we need at the dump."

"Sure," said Deputy Buddy. "The more the merrier. I hope you don't mind the smell."

"That's not a problem for me," P said, as he, M, and I boarded the horseless carriage. "Being struck by lightning twice has completely eliminated my sense of smell."

"P, you've been struck by lightning *a lot* more than twice," I told him. "In fact, I think it's happened close to thirty times."

He frowned.

"Really? Thirty times? I don't remember that. Hmmm. Maybe it's done something funny to my brain. Have I been acting strangely lately?"

M and I looked at each other for a moment before quickly shaking our heads.

"You? Strange? Never," I said.

"Not at all," M told him as she patted his spiky head. "You're the most normal man I've ever met."

Suddenly Aunt Dorcas came bolting out of the Baron Estate. For some reason, even though she had already eaten breakfast earlier, she was holding a hardboiled egg in each hand.[2]

"Where are you all going?" she demanded. "You never tell me when you go out, and that's really quite rude. What if I wanted to go out as well? Did you ever think about that? Maybe Aunt Dorcas wants to come too!"

"You're right, Dorcas," M said. "I apologize. We're going to the Pitchfork Desert Dump to search through the stinky trash to find parts for our new inventions. Would you like to join us?"

Aunt Dorcas's chin quivered. She sniffed the air and looked at the garbage carriage parked in front of our white picket fence.

"No," she said quietly. "But I appreciate the invitation."

With Buddy and Rose's carriage leading the way, we headed north in search of the Pitchfork Desert Dump. I was actually pretty excited. Sure, it would smell awful, but I knew that no one at school had ever been there before. Once they heard that I'd visited the dump with my family, they'd probably be begging me to describe it to them.

---

2. ?

When we got there, I realized there was only one word to describe it.

Stinky.

We could actually smell it when we were still a half mile away. There was a literal stink cloud hanging over the dump, a powerful stench that we could still smell even when we placed the clothespins over our noses.

I've smelled some pretty gross things in my life, but the Pitchfork Desert Dump takes the cake. In fact, it takes one of Rose's cakes.

Once we reached the dump and passed through the fence, we saw that her baked goods had their own little section at the far corner of the dump.

"Hmm, that's strange," Deputy Buddy said as he scratched his head. "Rose's pies and cakes weren't over in that corner the last time I was here."

"Maybe the rest of the garbage was so grossed out by Rose's baking, that it came to life and moved it over there," I suggested.

Rose picked up an empty bottle of Stone Lake Shoe Polish and threw it at me. It bounced off my head with a hollow sounding *ding*.

"Come on, Buddy," she said. "Let's dump the trash and then get out of here. I'll give you a hand with the heavy stuff."

P giggled like a weird kid in a candy store as he ran towards a collection of rusted metal and copper pipes, excited to find parts for his brilliant new invention that he had told the rest of us would be a terrific surprise.

"Remember, McLaron!" M called after him. "No more raccoons!"

"Of course not, Sharon!"

"And that means no raccoons dressed as other animals either."

"You never let me have any fun!"

I looked down and noticed that P had dropped something. When I leaned over to pick it up, I realized it was his *Listen Up, Stephen* Device. The red light at the end of it was blinking, which told me that it was still switched on. I was curious how the device worked, and so I stuck it in my ear.

I was almost knocked over by the intensity of sound. I could hear everything, and I mean *everything*.

I heard the wind blowing from miles away, and the horses from the trash carriage whinnying lightly as they napped.

I heard the clicking of the clockwork inside the horseless carriage. I heard my mother and father talking excitedly about a new invention as they sorted through the trash in search of something useful.

I heard the trash itself settling, metal creaking, papers crumbling, and Rose's pies and cakes making weird gurgling noises that I don't think food is supposed to make.

Then I turned and heard some new sounds, specifically the sounds of Rose and Deputy Buddy, having what they thought was a private conversation.

"Have you told them yet?"

"Not yet, Buddy. I don't know why, but I'm afraid to tell them."

"What are you afraid of? They're all such nice people."

"I know they are. They're like my family. In fact, they're more of a family to me than my *actual* family ever was. I guess that's why I'm afraid."

"Would you like me to tell them for you?"

"That's sweet of you, Buddy, but no. I should be the one to do it. I know it's silly for me to be scared to tell them because I'm certain they'll be happy for me. Happy for *us*, I mean."

"Of course they will. They really love you, Rose. And I do too. I'm the luckiest man in the world."

"I'm pretty lucky too. I think I'll tell them tonight over dinner."

"Am I invited?"

"Do you want to be?"

"That depends . . . will you be making dessert?"

I heard the sound of Rose punching Buddy on the arm.

"Ow! I'm just kidding, Rose."

"Watch it, Buddy Graham. You should be kinder to me. The only reason why I tried to learn how to bake a pie was to impress you. Just because I agreed to marry you doesn't mean that you can make fun of my cooking."

I gasped as I quickly turned away from them so they wouldn't know that I'd been spying. Rose was getting married? To doofy Buddy Graham? I couldn't believe it. It was the most shocking thing I'd ever heard. How would I be able to look at them without blurting out that I knew their secret? And what would happen once they got married? Would Rose move out of the Baron Estate? Would Buddy move in? Would she still work for my parents, or would she get a job working for the sheriff with Buddy?

I was so nervous and excited and confused by their conversation, that I almost missed the *Listen Up, Stephen* Device picking up the sound of something even crazier. At first it sounded like nothing more than a bunch of little squeaks, but, when I tilted my head closer to the pile of trash across from me, I was able to hear it more clearly:

"Good work, Sheriff Rattington and Deputy Ratty. The people of Ratville owe you a debt of gratitude for ridding our town of those rotten pies and cakes."

"Thank you. We were just doing our jobs, Mayor Ratberry."

"Who do you think it was that tried to poison our food with those awful baked goods?"

"Deputy Ratty and I discovered that it was the work of the dastardly Raterick Ratwood, the foulest villain in the world. He discovered the disgusting baked goods last month. He was planning on making us all sick from the nasty cakes and pies, so he could take over the town. But don't worry, sir. Raterick is now locked up in the Ratville Jailhouse, where he can't do us any more harm. He'll be stuck in there with the desert lice and fleas for a very long time."

"Excellent work! The people of Ratville are so grateful for what you've done, that they've requested that you and Deputy Ratty be the honorary guest judges at the annual Ratville Fair baking contest!"

"Gee, that sounds swell, Mayor Ratberry. Can we do it, Sheriff Rattington? Can we, huh?"

"Of course we can, Deputy Ratty. It would be an honor, Mayor Ratberry."

"The honor is all ours, Sheriff Rattington. The world needs more good rats like you."

I slowly pulled the *Listen Up, Stephen* Device out of my ear and placed it in my pocket. For a moment, I just stood there and stared at the ground.

"W.B.!" M called to me. "What's wrong? You look as though you've just seen a ghost."

I cleared my throat as I cast a quick glance at the pile of trash across from me.

"Nothing's wrong, M," I told her. "Everything's just hunky dory."

CERTIFIED BEANOLOGIST

Eric Bower is the author of The Bizarre Baron Inventions series. He was born in Denville, New Jersey, an event of which he has little recollection, yet the people who were there have repeatedly assured him that it happened. He currently lives in Pasadena, California. His favorite type of pasta is cavatappi, his favorite movie is *The Palm Beach Story*, and he is the proud recipient of a "Beanology Degree" from Jelly Belly University in Fairfield, California. His wife and family have told him that the degree is nothing to be proud of, since "It's not a real degree. You know that . . . Right?" and "Eric, they literally give them to everyone who visits the Jelly Belly factory," but he knows that they're all just jealous.

BRINGING WORDS TO LIFE

Agnieszka Grochalska lives in Warsaw, Poland. She received her MFA in Graphic Arts in 2014. Along the way, she explored traditional painting, printmaking, and sculpting, but eventually dedicated her keen eye and steady hand to drawing precise, detailed art reminiscent of classical storybook illustrations. Her current work is predominantly in digital medium, and has been featured in group exhibitions both in Poland and abroad.

She enjoys travel and cultural exchanges with people from around the world, blending those experiences with the Slavic folklore of her homeland in her works. When she isn't drawing or traveling, you can find her exploring the worlds of fiction in books and story-driven games.

Agnieszka's portfolio can be found at agroshka.com.